MISTRESS GUARD

LADY BLADE
BOOK ONE

CLARA WILS

Gryphon's Gate Publishing

Mistress Guard

Gryphon's Gate Publishing

550 King St. N.

PO Box 42088 Conestoga

Waterloo, ON

N2L 6K5

Print ISBN: 978-1-990587-55-9

CHAPTER 1

Tisera

I loved summers in Pearlia. I'd take the blazing sun over the dark chill days of winter in a heartbeat. And when storms did blow in off the Narrow Sea, the warm drenching rains kept lawns and gardens green and lush. Nights were comfortable and dawns came early, helping me to get up and get going, as I had today.

Having finished my morning calisthenics, I soaked in a bath, one of the few luxuries I'd afforded myself after the war. I'd purchased it with the heady payout for my service. The outside bathing area was hidden by a circular stand of juniper trees behind my cottage.

My cottage.

It still felt strange to think of the small dwelling and the land around it as mine, to think of myself as a landowner. This had all been purchased and built by my grandfather, who'd passed it down to my father, who'd passed it down to me.

The juniper grove had previously surrounded a private sitting area with three benches. I'd had them removed and the large wooden tub placed where they'd been. The gap between trees, where one entered the grove, I'd filled in with a stone archway holding a sturdy wooden door, for privacy.

The large tub had been made by the finest bath-makers in Pearlia. Wood had been bent and smoothed to form the sides and a bench within, on which I sat, the warm waters soothing away the aches I'd acquired through my vigorous workout. My head rested on a thick towel laid over the side of the large tub. I'd used harsh soaps and rough brushes to scrub myself raw and now — since I had nothing else of substance to do today — I luxuriated in the tepid waters.

And that's where Avela found me. I'd heard her calling, but my languid mind had not fully registered it.

"Mistress!" Avela said, hurrying through the doorway. "You must come at once! Master Kelric Drakoson is here and with him—"

I tuned out the rest.

Kel?

What in all the blazes of the deepest Hells was *he* doing here?

I hadn't spoken to him for almost a year now, not since his father had retired and handed command of Drako's Dragoons over to Kel. I'd been a part of Drako's mercenary company — and had great respect for the man — but I couldn't work for his son: that lying, untrustworthy piece of shit. So, I'd left and we'd not spoken since. What was he doing here now?

"Mistress, did you hear me? I said, Master Kelric Drakoson is here and Prince Victor is with him!"

Wait, what?

The crown-prince?

I shot up out of the bath, grabbing my towel to cover myself, as if the two men were standing in the doorway, which they weren't.

Thank the gods.

My mind reeled.

"Fuck me," I hissed. "The crown prince? Here?"

"Yes, mistress! Please, they're asking for you."

I stepped onto the bench, then over the side of the tub and down the steps built into the outside of the basin to help get in and out. Wrapping the towel around myself, I got as far as the stone-laid path and stopped dead.

"Fuck." I couldn't return to the cottage like this. "Fuck, fuck, fuck, FUCK!"

Avela flinched at my language. The girl — no, she was my age, I had to stop thinking of her that way — was a gentle soul.

"Mistress?"

All I had with me were my soiled work-out clothes and the towel. Usually, I'd have worn just the towel for the short trip back to the cottage to dress. But I couldn't do that with the fucking prince waiting for me!

"Avela, run and fetch me some clothes from my wardrobe. Tell the prince..." *what?* That I was in the bath? That didn't sound good, but it was probably better than lying and would excuse a bit of a delay and fuss on my part. So, yeah... "Tell the prince I was bathing and will need a moment. Master Kel and the prince can wait in the cottage for me."

Luckily my housemate, Dazar — a man who was like a brother to me — was off in the inner city on an errand. He shouldn't be back before noon. That would leave the cottage empty and quiet for Kel and the prince.

Avela started to run off, but I stopped her with a word. "Wait."

"Yes, mistress?"

"Make sure to get my blue shirt and the black pants," I specified.

Avela nodded and ran off.

I dried myself quickly, thankful I'd recently chopped back my hair. It dried much faster — and it wouldn't get in my way in a fight — even if it *was* a spikey mess that never settled the way I wished.

I stood there, naked, waiting for Avela to return and wondering what in the blazes of the Five Hells the prince was doing here... and with Kel no less.

I heard Avela's running sandals on the stone path before the door to the bathing area was yanked open and slammed shut.

"The prince and Master Kelric are waiting in the cottage, here are the clothes you requested." She held out the bundle, neatly folded and pristine. She was out of breath, sweaty and frazzled, but she'd come through for me. I was eternally grateful.

I dressed quickly.

"How do I look?" I asked Avela.

She smiled. "Far better than I do, I'm sure."

I tried not to grimace at that. As much as I was composed and she was a bit winded, Avela was a beautiful girl — no, *woman* — with all of the curves men loved. She possessed a full, high bust, slender waist and arms, round hips and thighs, bouncing blond curls, and stunning sunrise-golden eyes.

I — on the other hand — had none of that.

I was tall for a woman and built like a man: strong and sturdy, with square shoulders, thick strong arms and legs, straight hips, a narrow waist and a bust with which I had a complicated relationship.

I certainly wasn't full-bosomed like Avela, which might have been nice, if I'd ever wanted to look womanly. Yet I also wasn't completely flat, which would have been great when wearing armor. I was large enough that my breasts always ached and chafed after being in armor too long, but not large enough to fill out most dresses. Not that I wore a lot of dresses. Under a shirt, I looked like I had the chest of a very muscular man, if a bit more rounded. Not womanly at all. It was a good thing I rarely wore dresses or wanted to be womanly.

But that didn't mean I didn't want a man in my life. However, if my build didn't scare off men, my scars did. I was a warrior and scars came with the job.

Luckily, this blue shirt — my best shirt — was loose and billowy, hiding a lot of my masculine features. The black pants were just a bit tight and showed off my muscular legs. That was unintentional. They were meant to be loose and straight, but I'd bulked up a bit since I'd first bought them.

I was ready.

"Thank you, Avela," I said, leaving her as I headed to the door, but I stopped with my hand on the latch. "Thank you... for everything. I couldn't run this place without you and Shorine."

It was true. I wasn't one for gardening nor tending to lands. My father had hired Shorine to do those jobs and I'd kept her on. The woman was growing old though and had recently 'adopted' Avela to be her successor. Avela had taken to the job eagerly, mostly helping Shorine but sometimes being a lady's maid for me... on the rare occasion I felt like being a lady.

I left the bath and walked to the cottage, trying to keep calm as my mind and emotions raged within me.

I stopped at the door to the cottage and took a long, deep breath before entering, a pleasant smile on my face... for the prince only.

Kel could choke on a cherry pit and die for all I cared.

I entered and the two men rose from the small sitting area at one end of the open main room. I knelt and bowed my head. "Your Highness," I said with due reverence.

"Please rise," Victor said, his tone full and commanding. Though it wasn't as deep and resonant as Kel's.

I did so.

"How may I serve you," I asked, incredibly curious.

I kept my gaze focused on the prince. I daren't even glance at Kel. Looking at that man for too long would get me flustered and furious at the same time. Gods, but he was a handsome man, and a lying, betraying bastard. I didn't want to think about our torrid nights during the siege of Vestrea, nor how he'd abandoned me after the war.

The prince, on the other hand, was quite pleasant to look at. The man was tall and had a regal bearing, with square shoulders on a lean, strong frame. He possessed a slightly protruding chin, aqua-blue eyes, and flaxen-blond hair. The entire royal family, and most of the nobility of Pearlia, possessed similar features — jewel-toned eyes and blond hair — some wearing them better than others. The prince wore his very well indeed.

"Kelric tells me you are a hardened warrior, yes?" I didn't have time to answer before he went on: "Fought in the Ero-Pearlian War, and distinguished yourself? And that you can be trusted to be discreet?"

I waited to see if he'd say more. When he didn't, I nodded. "Yes, your highness."

Still, I didn't know what he'd need with me specifically. There were many veterans of that war. Though the bit about being "discreet" had piqued my curiosity even more.

The prince drew a long breath and looked at Kel. Inadvertently, my gaze followed his and I took in all of Kel's glorious manliness.

The untrustworthy, deserting cad was brutishly handsome. The lustrous deep brown of his skin denoted his non-Pearlian heritage. His father — Drako — had been full Usovi, but Kel's mother had been a Pearlian woman, which meant Kel didn't share Drako's ebony complexion. He was tall and hung like a prized stallion...

Did I say 'hung'? I meant built.

He was built like a prized stallion, with massive

rolling shoulders and heavy slabs of muscle for a chest. Even after a year, he was still *extremely* fit, his shirt falling over his form, not bulging over his belly like I had secretly hoped it might. It looked like the semi-retirement of working for the crown hadn't softened him yet.

He kept his head shaved — a custom of the Usovi — and had deep, dark eyes. A rigid nose and full lips over a strong chin anchored his look as all man and all warrior.

Seeing him again flared my rage, even as my core clenched with heated moisture. My body's betrayal made me hate him all the more.

"Captain Drakoson has recommended you for a special mission," the prince said.

I barely heard him, my confused emotions billowing to almost unmanageable levels. I dragged my attention back to the prince, which wasn't easy, but once I did, I managed to calm myself.

"Did he?" I was more than a little stunned by this.

"It's not something any of his... *men* can do," the prince said, and instantly I understood.

"Ah, yes." I nodded. "Go on."

As a woman warrior, I was a rare breed. The only one with any real experience and skill in the city... perhaps in the entire kingdom. Usually it meant I missed out on opportunities, most employers preferring a swordsman over a swordswoman, but in this case, apparently it was a boon. A rare instance indeed. I still didn't know what the prince wanted, but things were quickly being narrowed down.

As my mind worked to figure out what it could be, the

prince grew a bit awkward and hesitant. He cleared his throat.

"I... ah... have need of a guard, for a woman... *friend* of mine."

"With all respect Your Highness, it's probably best if you tell her everything," Kel said. His deep voice sent a shock of remembrance through me. I recalled how he'd whispered in my ear as we'd lain exhausted in each other's arms, his thick, pulsing cock still heavy inside me after a moment of passion, stolen from the night.

Clenching my jaw, I dispelled those thoughts and listened.

The prince cleared his throat again. This time he was slightly more forthright. "You may have heard I've taken a mistress."

I had, but only in passing. I didn't really follow the lives of the royals.

He sighed heavily. "I..." He licked his lips and decided not to say whatever that had been. Instead he drew a breath and started again.

"My mother has forbidden me to see the woman."

I didn't blame the queen. Prince Victor was a married man with three children, one of whom — Princess Anastasia — was nearly a grown woman herself at fourteen. And his wife, Princess Kira, was from Ossara and any infidelity could hinder our relations with that neighboring nation. It was quite the scandal that Victor had taken up with some unknown woman at a palace ball.

The prince squared his shoulders. "But I am a grown man and I will do as I wish. I love Veora and she loves me. And though it might damn me, I will see her again!" The vehemence with which he said this startled me. He must truly love this woman, even if that made him a cheating bastard like Kel. Not that I would say anything to the prince.

He continued, "Yet I am under constant scrutiny and I cannot leave the palace without guards and a procession most days. I was lucky to make it here with just Captain Drakoson today, and that required special planning. Hence, I cannot sneak out to go to her."

The pieces were falling into place.

"So," the prince said, resuming a more neutral tone, "I require someone who is discreet and capable to escort and protect my beloved and sneak her into the palace to be with me. I will give you all the information you need to get past the guards at the servant's gate, but you will not be able to carry any weapons, nothing larger than a dagger. Kelric assures me you are more than capable at unarmed combat. As well, I will let you know of secret passages within the palace you can use to get her to my rooms. I will be entrusting you not only with royal secrets but the life of my beloved. So... can you do this for me, Tisera Halvensdaughter?"

Could I? Yes.

Would I?

Helping an immoral prince and his lover on the word of my bastard ex-lover? I didn't know.

The real question was: did I have a choice?

CHAPTER 2

Tisera

No, I didn't.

I was broke.

The last two months I'd only just managed to pay the land taxes on my not-so-small plot within the city. Last month I'd had to borrow a bit of money from my house-mate Dazar. He was more than willing — and more than capable — of paying for everything I needed, but I hated having to ask for his help, or *anyone's* help.

I hadn't worked in months and I desperately needed a job. So, I didn't really have a choice. Even if it hadn't been a prince asking — to whom one does not say "no" — I'd have taken any job which came my way.

"I can and I will, Your Highness." I nodded my head solemnly.

He approached and extended his hand. Most contracts for a mercenary like me would be in writing, but this one would be by handshake only. I took his hand, clasping my hand around his wrist, and he took mine. We shook firmly.

I shot a look over the prince's shoulder at Kel, which I hoped said: *thank you for this opportunity*, while also saying: *I hope you rot in the deepest of Hells, you bastard*. It was a complicated look.

"Tell me everything," I said as the prince released my wrist and I motioned for him to sit again.

Instead, he shook his head. "Why don't we speak in my carriage, I'll take you to meet Veora so you know where she lives and I can introduce you two."

"As you wish, Your Highness." I motioned to the door. He left and Kel followed behind him by a few steps.

"You're welcome," Kel whispered, tone even and a bit cold.

I wanted to hit him, or better yet, plant a well-placed kick between his legs, but I didn't. The fact was, he *had* helped me, even if it seemed he hadn't truly wanted to. He also hadn't had much of a choice. If the prince had asked for recommendations for female warriors... I was the only one.

And it wouldn't look good for me to be picking a fight in front of the prince. But by Brovos, I wanted to give Kel a good thrashing. Though a small part of me was a bit worried if I began grappling with him... it would turn into something else once our bodies were pressed together. So, best not to think of that... for many reasons.

I closed up the house and quickly told Avela I'd be out for a bit then followed the others out to a carriage. Kel held the door for me like the gentleman he wasn't. I was a bit surprised when he didn't join us. Instead, he closed the door behind me and probably joined the driver or took up the footman's position at the back. It was just the prince and I inside.

The carriage started rolling down my long laneway.

"You and Kel have a history." It wasn't a question.

"We do." I didn't feel like elaborating. What I could say was, "He is an exceptional warrior, loyal and dedicated to Pearlia." *If not loyal and dedicated to women.*

"He said something similar about you. Your father was a mercenary in his father's service?"

"Yes." It had been four years since my father had died, but it hadn't been the war that had killed him. "The waning sickness took him."

The prince grimaced. "I'm sorry. That is... unfortunate. I'm sure you know my sister, Princess Alice, had the waning sickness and though she survived, she is still frail and weak to this day."

I nodded. "Yes. In fact, my Aunt Emri is Princess Alice's lady's maid."

The prince nodded and smiled warmly. "I didn't know that. Emri has been a wonderful blessing for Alice; for us all. She takes excellent care of my sister."

I returned the smile. I knew Emri was happy in her position.

My aunt had raised me for a time. I'd not known my mother. She'd died giving birth to me. My father had been off serving in the Dath-Riven War, so Aunt Emri had taken me in. But when I'd been seven, Emri had taken the position as Alice's lady's maid and the war had ended. I had been raised by my father after that.

All he'd known was a mercenary's life, and that was what he'd taught me. I'd been a hardened campaigner by the time I was ten. I'd been able to wield a sword as well as any boy my age by twelve and had been officially apprenticed to my father the next year... along with Kel. My father had joined with Drako's Dragoons when I'd been eleven. He'd proven himself and Drako had liked him, so he'd given his son to my father as an apprentice. That had been how Kel and I had gotten to know each other, and why we knew each other so well. As for why we hated each other, that had come later.

"Now, to business," the prince said, and I listened intently. "In truth, I am not worried about my mother's condemnation of my lover. She won't stop me from seeing Veora. She had to say what she did to save face, politically. But that also means Veora cannot be seen in the palace openly, hence the secrecy. Also, since it is fairly well known that Veora is my mistress, there will always be the constant threat of danger from those who seek to hurt me, or perhaps ransom her freedom. I offered her security at all times, but she is content with the protection of her brother most of the time. They live together, she and her brother. His name is Merik. Hence, she'd be most vulnerable when alone, like when she's coming to the palace to visit me. She has reluctantly agreed to a guard at such times, as long as it is a woman."

"So, I would only be needed when she's coming to the palace, no other times?" I asked.

"That would be up to her. If she asks for an escort at any time, I would expect you to oblige."

Which meant I could be called upon day or night. I

hoped this paid well, though I didn't ask about money. Hopefully, the prince would get to that.

And he did. "For such a service, knowing it might take you away from your family or other duties at any hour, I would pay you two strips per week, for a total of a hundred strips per year or two royals."

I tried not to gawk. One strip — a bar of silver roughly the length of one's palm — was a significant payment in itself. Two a week, would mean I'd easily be able to pay my monthly taxes and have a small fortune left over. I'd be a very wealthy woman after a year of this, assuming the relationship lasted that long. I'd be able to pay my taxes for — I did the math quickly — another five years if I didn't find work.

I nodded solemnly. That would be more than enough pay for the inconvenience of having to escort this woman around at her every whim. "You are very generous," I said and meant it.

He nodded. "Just... keep her safe," he said softly.

I couldn't get over how much he seemed to care for this woman, or that he had a mistress at all. I hadn't thought anyone in the royal family would be like that. As much as they had all married for politics, not love, they had all made the best of it, or so I'd thought.

We rode in silence as the city passed by.

I lived in the second ring of the city. My grandfather had been a merchant wealthy enough to buy this plot of land from a destitute noble who'd been selling off his holdings.

The inner ring — or first ring — of Pearlia had been the original city, established when Aestrian settlers had found this protected harbor after their arduous journey across the Narrow Sea. Many of the original buildings had long since been replaced with the marble and stone structures of The Pearl Palace, The Grand Market, The Forum, and many nobles' houses.

The second ring — known as The Gardens — had originally been where the early nobility had built manors "outside" the city with vast lawns and gardens. Eventually a second city wall had been built, encompassing the second ring, and as the nobility moved out or went bankrupt, those vast estates had been bought up and divided into smaller, but still luxurious, plots for wealthy merchants and such.

The carriage passed under the wall, through a gatehouse, into the third ring, where most of the citizens of Pearlia lived. Off of the main road were narrow lane-ways and dark alleys shadowed by the seemingly outward-leaning, jettied buildings.

People teemed through this part of the city, making way for our carriage as well as other carts and wagons. I was a bit surprised when we exited the city itself through the West Gate, rolling out into the countryside. Slums huddled close around the city wall. Past them was the caravansary, a large area for foreign traders and merchants — or anyone seeking passage elsewhere — to meet and load or unload wares. Within the caravansary was The New Market, where merchants could buy and sell without needing to get passes into the city itself. The mass of brightly colored stalls and handcarts seemed more than usually busy this morning; a caravan must have arrived recently. Farther out from the city, beyond the market, were farms and the newer nobles' estates.

It was down the lane of one of the smaller estates which we turned. This would be a decent walk for me, probably a good half-an-hour each way from my house.

The manor itself wasn't large, situated on a beautiful — if not large — plot of land next to the Pearline River.

The carriage stopped and Kel opened the door for the prince and me. The prince nodded for me to exit first. I did, ignoring Kel's hand to help me down.

As the prince descended from the carriage, a woman came running out from the house in a flurry of pale pink skirts. As she raced by me, I caught only her most notable features: a long cascade of hair — like flowing red wine — streaming behind her, a pale face with large green eyes gleaming like emeralds, and full red lips.

When she finally stopped, throwing her arms around the prince and covering his face with kisses, I took in the rest of her. If what I'd overheard from my male companions during my days in Drako's Dragoons held any weight, the woman had ideal proportions. I didn't know if her dress had a corset to it, but if not then she had a natural hour-glass figure with full hips and bosom and a slender waist and long legs. I could see how a man might become infatuated with her.

She pressed her lips to the prince's for a long and — very steamy — kiss. The prince was just a little flushed when they finally separated. He cleared his throat. "Ah, Master Drakoson, and Tisera Halvensdaughter, may I introduce Veora Thistledown."

The woman turned to us, beaming with a large smile.

"It is a pleasure to meet you," she said eagerly. "Any friend of Victor's is a friend of mine."

I wasn't a "friend" of the prince, I was working for him, but I nodded.

"Lady Thistledown, I am Tisera. I will be escorting you from now on whenever you wish to be out and about in the city, and particularly when you are going to meet Prince Victor."

"Oh!" she exclaimed with a clap of her hands. "That's wonderful. I'm sure we'll become fast friends!"

I was less sure.

I didn't much care for the frivolity of other women. I'd been raised as a warrior. I felt awkward around girlish women, perhaps because I saw what I might have become... and was horrified by it. I'd much rather have a sword in my hand than a flower.

Still, I let Veora embrace me, holding me close. She practically hummed with joy and life and after a moment I relented a little, easing.

"I'm sure we shall get to know each other well," I said softly.

"Yes, we shall!" she said and released me. Then she curtseyed to Kel.

"Master," she said with respect. When she leaned forward in her curtsey, it gave Kel a good view of her full bosom exposed by the low neckline of her dress.

He seemed a bit stunned, then shook it off. "Ah... Lady, it is I who should be bowing to you," Kel said.

True. She was nobility and he wasn't. He bowed low and when he came up, the stoic hardness to his features had returned.

"Will you be escorting me as well?" she asked Kel, then turned to the prince. "I'd asked for just a woman."

Kel replied. "Ah, no, I will not. Tisi will be more than enough to keep you safe." He caught his use of my nickname and corrected himself quickly. "That is Sera— I mean Tisera."

Kel cleared his throat, giving himself a moment to regain his composure. "She is an excellent warrior but dress her up right and no one would know it."

He glanced at me, and I guessed he was imagining me in Veora's dress. I couldn't imagine myself in that low-cut, frilly, pink monstrosity, but Kel gave a half smile, a quick breath of a laugh then was all stony features again.

"Tisi?" Veora said, turning to me. "What a wonderful name. I shall call you Tisi, if I may?"

"You may," I said grudgingly. I wasn't going to deny her in front of the prince, even though that name was reserved for those who knew me well. I got the feeling she'd know me well soon enough. We'd be spending a lot of time together.

"Then it is set," the prince said softly. "Tisera, thank you for this. I shall have someone drop off payment for the first three months in advance tomorrow."

That would be nice.

Then came some talk about when I'd come to see Veora next and the schedule which she and the prince would be keeping. I'd be returning on the morrow to escort Veora to the New Market, outside the city. The day after, I'd take her to see the prince.

"Come on, Sera, let's go," Kel said — using the nickname I despised — pulling me aside with a bit more force than he needed to. I didn't know why until he whispered. "The prince will be remaining here for a while to 'wet his whistle,' so we're walking back to the city."

Ah.

"Perhaps, but we won't be doing it together." I tore my arm from his iron grip. "You go ahead."

Kel grunted, jaw tight. "Right."

He said a few quiet words to the prince, then left.

I loitered as the prince and Veora headed to the swathe of gardens between the house and the river. I quickly lost sight of them among the hedges and trees.

Something caught my eye and I looked to see a shadow in the open doorway of the small manor-house. A man in finely tailored dark clothing glared at me. This would be Merik, the brother, I assumed. There was nothing friendly about him. In fact, I instantly disliked him, getting a cold feeling from him. He wasn't one to mess with.

I nodded to him. He glared back before retreating into the manor and closing the door.

A shiver ran down my spine as I waited another few long breaths — so my long legs wouldn't catch up with Kel as I returned to the city — then turned and began a slow walk home.

This job would be... interesting.

At least I would be well paid to be a glorified nanny.

My fortunes had turned in an instant. Though I wondered, offhand, if they had actually changed for better... or worse.

CHAPTER 3

KELRIC

SEEING TISI AGAIN AFTER ALL THIS TIME HAD GOTTEN ME all twisted up: furious and heated and wistful all at once.

I needed to get my emotions settled before I returned to my troops. The Dragoons had a commission with the crown now, we were on the queen's payroll — which was how Prince Victor had found me — and that meant keeping things running smoothly for the nearly five-hundred men under my command. I couldn't show weakness and I couldn't be distracted by women.

Especially Tisi.

"Sera," I muttered with a grin. She hated that name. She always had. It was Tisera or Tisi or nothing. Though her adopted brother — Dazar — called her 'Dizzy' and she didn't seem to mind. But I'd taken to calling her Sera in my thoughts, knowing she despised the short form.

And I'd do anything I could to make her pay for what she'd done to me.

I ground my teeth at the memory — it was seared into my brain as much as I wanted to forget it — of her straddling Sergeant Tomas, moaning and crying out, stinking of sweat and sex. I'd only seen her from the back as I'd peeked through the doorway, but that had been more than enough. She'd cheated on me. And to think I'd been ready to marry her!

Gods! That still burned my soul. How could she?

I tried to distract myself by remembering Prince Victor's new mistress. She was all woman, round and ready, beautiful in a lively and energetic way. I could see why he might have broken the bond with his wife for the woman. She was certainly intoxicating. If I hadn't known better, I'd have thought the curtsey she'd given me was some sly seduction. Not only had she displayed her abundance of cleavage, but she'd paused long enough to swell them with a deep breath. Lady Thistledown was a dangerous beauty indeed. Yet... she wasn't one to marry.

For that, I'd want a woman more like me...

More like Tisi.

I ground my teeth again. I hated that woman nearly as much as I still loved her. The trouble was, I couldn't seem to rid myself of my feelings for her. I'd meant to marry her and she'd gone and bedded the first man she'd seen — other than me — after the war. How could she do that to me? I thought she'd been the one.

I...

I had to stop thinking of her.

I hadn't realized how much seeing her again would burn me.

She hadn't changed. She was blistering fire and pent-up power, ready to be unleashed upon her foes. And I was a foe now.

I didn't know what I'd done to cause her to betray me, if anything at all, but she seemed to hate me as much as I hated her and I couldn't figure out why. I wasn't the one who'd slept with our unit leader.

Seeing her today had nearly been too much for me. The shifting silk of that dark-blue shirt over her lithe and athletic form and those pants clinging to her strong legs had almost made me burst forth from my pants. Thankfully, my lust had been tempered by my loathing. As much as I didn't want to, all I had to do was remember her and Sergeant Tomas together and I lost all desire for her.

Almost all.

And rehashing it all was *not* helping me relax. My muscles bunched in growing tension. Perhaps I should visit a whore before I returned to my men. Though, given how I was feeling I didn't think that would go well. I'd probably get some slight and waifish girl and nearly break her with the force I wished to release.

That's why Tisi had been so amazing. She was strong and hardy. I didn't have to restrain myself with her, and she certainly hadn't restrained herself with me. Together we'd been... amazing and powerful.

Fuck. I was doomed.

I couldn't get her out of my mind.

By the time I stormed into the massive barracks compound for the Dragoons I was in a foul mood. I quickly undressed from the finery I'd donned for Prince Victor's visit and put on my battle armor. I wouldn't normally train in all of this, but I wanted to go all out and exhaust myself so I could forget today.

Marching into the practice yard, I plucked up a practice sword and went to town on one of the wooden dummies. Hacking it to pieces over the course of... well, I lost track of time. All I knew was I was a sweaty, aching, tired, and burned-out mess when I finished.

And everyone else in the yard stared at me.

I left, hoping to sleep through the rest of the day after a hot bath, but a page found me as I returned to my room.

"Sir, a noble gentleman is here to see you," the page said, voice breaking, rising through multiple tones, as the poor young man fought to keep his fear of me in check. I must have been some sight: a heavily armored, sweaty, raging, mess of a man.

"The prince?" I asked quickly, a bit too harshly.

The page flinched. "No, sir. I do not believe he is a prince, just a nobleman. He says his name is Lord Leomund of Seven Stars."

I grunted. I wanted to tell his entitled ass to go away, but with my commission for the crown, that wouldn't look good. I could refuse a nobleman since I was working for the royals specifically, but I should at least hear the man out first, *then* refuse them in person.

"He's in the sitting room," the page said, probably seeing my hesitation.

I nodded. "Thank you," I said, with a heavy sigh.

I stalked — still a sweaty, stinking mess — to the space we'd set aside for visitors. It was a large well-appointed room with a great hearth, many comfortable chairs and couches, and an extensive, if not extravagant drink tray.

The lord was looking at the array of swords hung on the wall. He had a slender and dainty appearance, which made me think of him as young, though he was probably my age. He turned at my arrival, probably hearing me in my heavy armor. His bright green eyes widened upon seeing me.

"Oh!" he exclaimed. "Are we to begin at once then?"

"Begin?" I was thrown by this, and that only added to my frustration and anger.

I was probably just a little too harsh when I demanded, "Who are you? What do you want?" Though the more I looked at him, the more I recognized him. But then... with their uniform blond hair and jewel-tone eyes, all the nobles and royals of Pearlia looked like him.

The tall, lanky man took a step back, shocked.

"Apologies," he said with a faint nod. "I assumed my message was passed on to you. I had told the young man who brought me here that I wished to receive combat training. My name is—"

"Leomund of Seven Stars, I know. That much did get passed on." The poor page had probably forgotten the rest when he'd seen me as I was. And with everything else that had happened today, I couldn't help but laugh, a good long hearty guffaw. This twig of a man wanted combat training? I'd break him in half if I went against him.

He was a dandy, who clearly didn't know one end of a sword from the other. He wasn't worth my time... but... I suddenly had a great idea.

I grinned. "I've got just the person you should see."

CHAPTER 4

Leonin

I left the Dragoon's compound feeling a little shaken. I'd heard of the infamous Kelric Drakoson — even seen him across large banquet halls from time to time — but hadn't expected him to be quite so imposing and *filthy* up close.

He wasn't taller than me, but somehow in that heavy armor of his, he'd seemed to loom over me. It was not something I was used to. Hopefully this Sera he was sending me to see would be a bit more of a pleasant sight. I was uncertain about taking combat lessons from a woman but given what I'd gone through so far... that might be my only option.

The trouble was my name. And it wasn't the name I'd given Kelric: Leomund of Seven Stars. My true name was Prince Leonin Pearlece.

I'd had to use the pseudonym with Kelric since he worked for my family. He'd know that we princes had royal combat trainers. He'd also know that training me would be a huge liability for him and have refused instantly... as had everyone else I'd talked to.

Yet, since we'd never formally met, I'd hoped to convince him I wasn't a royal, but from a high noble family. The Seven Stars family was well respected, but still, Kelric hadn't wished to take me on. And he'd been my last hope... until he'd given me another name: Sera.

As for why I needed an instructor... it had all begun six years ago, when I'd married Lady Theodora of Vestrea.

I sighed heavily. She had been a good woman. I had come to respect her, even if I hadn't loved her. But our *very* political marriage had started a war. Vestrea had been a province of Eromore, a neighboring kingdom to the north, and the marriage hadn't been sanctioned by the Eromorn King. Which meant, Pearlia had subtly annexed the province and Eromore had gone to war to retake it.

Many had died because of our marriage, but Theodora had always remained certain and sure that our marriage had been the correct course for her and her nation. She firmly believed that Vestrea belonged with Pearlia, not Eromore. She'd had a warrior's heart, stalwart in her faith and the justness of her cause. It had inspired me.

I'd always loved books more than blades. I'd been taught weapons, as had all the royal children, but I'd had no talent for it. I'd often skipped weapons training to sneak off to the library and delve into the ancient tales of gods and heroes.

I'd much preferred reading about battle to fighting, but Theodora's fierce nature had started to sway me.

Then she'd died in childbirth two years into our marriage. The baby hadn't survived either. I'd vowed to her, on her deathbed, I'd become a man worthy of her warrior's spirit.

Her death had also meant the end of the war, since the Pearlian claim over Vestrea had vanished. An armistice had been called. Pearlia had come away with the city of Vestrea — almost completely destroyed by the war — and some surrounding countryside, which made up the southern-most portion of the province. The rest of the province had returned to Eromore.

I'd mourned Theodora for a year, as was right. After that my mother, the Queen, had come to me and told me, in no uncertain terms, I'd be joining the priesthood. An unmarried son was no use to her and she could see how I had no desire to marry again. The first marriage had caused enough trouble.

It had seemed a reasonable course for me, given my more studious nature, but I couldn't fulfil my vow to Theodora in the priesthood.

Yet my vow didn't change that I'd always been poor at combat. What it changed was my dedication to learn, to grow, no matter what it took. I rededicated myself and my life to the study of weapons.

But when my mother had found out I'd been seeking

combat training, she'd banned all the palace trainers and guards from working with me. She remained adamant I should enter the priesthood.

Thus began a very long quest to find a teacher. Yet, I was too well known. No mercenary captain or guard captain of another noble house would risk training me. If they accidentally hurt me, they'd be in deep trouble with my mother. I'd spent three years sneaking out of the palace when I could, feigning some interest in the priesthood for my mother, all the while seeking a combat instructor.

Kelric had been my last hope.

Now, this Sera was my last hope.

I found her home and stopped at the side of the road to admire it. It seemed a pleasant place, indicating a certain level of wealth. A long front lawn stretched from the road to the small cottage. A low, rough stone wall separated it from the next plot on the one side. The laneway, guarded by two straight lines of trees on either side of it, stretched down the other side of the lawns. Behind the cottage there were some other buildings and what looked like some gardens and small bits of forested areas. It looked quaint and lovely.

I grew increasingly curious about the warrior-woman who lived here. Was she some minor noblewoman who'd learned swordplay, or perhaps a woman who'd worked her way up in the army until she'd earned enough to retire here?

Was she older?

Was she—?

"Can I help you?"

The voice startled me from my reverie. I looked to see a woman next to me with a questioning glance on her long, squarish face. Her brown hair was cut incredibly short, sweeping down over her forehead and left eye but otherwise standing in tufts and spikes. Her brown eyes were hard, one brow raised. She seemed a bit abrasive and standoffish.

She cocked her head to one side and added: "Is there a reason you're staring at my house?"

Her house?

Was *this* Sera?

She was so young! For some reason I'd assumed she must be at least in her forties, if not elderly. I also assumed that was why I'd never heard of her, if she'd been granted status as a noble or granted this land before I was born, but this woman... She looked to be no older than thirty.

Caught off guard, I stammered, which wasn't like me at all. I finally managed to eke out the words: "I'm Leo."

"I'm Tisera. I repeat, can I help you with something?"

Tisera, not Sera, interesting. Perhaps she was the daughter of the woman I sought?

But again, words stuck in my throat. When they did come, they were utterly ridiculous: "I want to fight... with... your mother?"

The woman's confused and questioning look grew more pronounced and a bit disgusted. "My mother is long dead, *good sir*." Her inflection suggested that I was not — in fact — a *good sir* and vexing her.

Her mother was dead, but then...

"Are you Sera?" I asked.

Her face turned hard. "Don't call me that." She turned and began stalking toward the laneway. But she stopped after only a few paces, her head cocking further to one side. "Did Kel send you?"

Kel? Oh... Kelric Drakoson. "Ah... yes."

Without turning she asked. "You want to fight me?" Her shoulder lurched in what I guessed was a laugh. I wasn't sure that was entirely called for.

"I want to learn to fight," I said, finally managing to get out the right words.

Those same shoulders fell a little with a sigh perhaps. "Ah." She turned back. "You're noble, yes?"

I nodded.

Good, she hadn't figured out who I really was.

"Too much coin for your own good, sort of noble?"

I quirked a smile. That was definitely true. "Yes."

She looked me up and down as if I were some aged nag of a horse she was considering buying. "Do you have any experience with a sword?"

"Some." I quickly added: "But, assume I know nothing, I'd start from the beginning."

She raised a brow at that. "Good, you're that smart at least." She gave another heavy sigh. "I don't usually train others, so my rates are high. One strip. How's that sound?"

A strip of silver? That was nothing. "For how many sessions?"

She laughed. "One."

Ah... well this could add up then, but that didn't matter. "Done."

She seemed surprised, but then nodded. "Come this way, good sir Leo." She turned and began walking down the laneway.

I hurried to catch up.

She was tall for a woman. I only just looked over the top of her head so my long legs could easily keep pace with hers, but still, she walked briskly.

Without looking she asked, "Leo. That's a common name for your generation of nobles, isn't it? Named after the Young Prince?"

Young Prince indeed. I was twenty-and-five years of age!

But what she'd said was true and why I could get away with using at least part of my real name. "Yes, I'm Leomund of Seven Stars, but you can call me Leo if you like."

"Done. Leo. I've never liked formalities anyway." She glanced over at me. "I'm assuming you didn't bring any clothes for fighting?"

No, I hadn't. "Are we beginning now?"

"Yes. I want to test you. You up for it?"

Someone had finally agreed to teach me, I didn't want to lose that. "Of course. Whatever you desire, I will oblige."

Her one brow raised again. "Indeed?" We walked in silence down the long laneway. "I will want to get changed before we begin. Do you have time to wait?"

Everyone thought I was at the Library of Wisteri, but I'd slipped out the back. I had all day if I wanted it.

"Yes." My heart began to beat faster. I was finally going to begin my training. Though... Perhaps I shouldn't be too excited as she only said she would test me. Did that mean she might still turn me away? I had to impress her.

"Wait here," she said when we reached the yard behind the house. She continued on to the small cottage and went inside.

I looked around. A large barn stood to my right, from within came the bleat of sheep. That must have been how she kept that large lawn out-front so well-tended. Beside the barn was a large garden, stretching away toward the back of the property. On the other side of that was a stand of decorative trees, including a copse of closely planted junipers, which oddly had a stone arch and wooden doorway on one side. Paths led back to other shade trees and sitting areas toward the back of the property as well.

Very quaint.

An elderly woman emerged from the barn and stopped when she saw me. "You here to see the mistress? She's out, gone off with—"

"I am yes, and she just returned, I believe."

The old woman nodded. "Good, so you're sorted?"

"Yes, thank you."

She nodded and went toward the gardens.

Odd.

Tisera emerged from the cottage a moment later wearing what looked like a padded gambeson, with more sedate clothes beneath than the dark blue and black she'd been wearing before. She held two swords made of wood and threw one at me. My reflexes were quick enough that I was able to catch it and she seemed surprised. "Not bad."

"I may not know how to fight, but that doesn't mean I'm an awkward clod," I clarified.

She nodded. "Point taken." She set herself in a fighting stance, lifting her sword. "Defend yourself."

I thought to ask: "Do I get any padding?"

"Not until you've earned it. Pass your test first."

That was clear enough. I expected I was about to be in considerable pain. But, since I did know some basics, I held the sword as I'd been taught and set myself.

She tilted her head to one side then the other observing me, quirking her lips. I couldn't tell if that was a good sign or not.

Then she attacked: a blur. My sword went flying.

I yelped. My hand ached from the force of having the sword torn away. In addition, she'd hit me twice. My right shoulder throbbed with a stinging ache and my side was going to have one Hells of a nasty bruise.

I stumbled back and unceremoniously fell on my ass.

Tisera had reset to her ready stance and for an instant, I wondered if she had moved at all. Perhaps it had been some trick. She might be a Phorasti, with mystical powers. But that seemed less likely than the possibility of her just being incredibly quick and skilled with a blade.

"Get up," she said, hard, stern.

I did. "I'm assuming I failed the test then?" I said dusting myself off, trying not to wince as I moved my right arm.

She chuckled, a bit of a hard edge to it. "Pick up the sword," she said.

That wasn't an answer.

"I'm not sure if I can. My hand is half-numb." I picked up the practice weapon with my left hand and flexed my right hand a few times before gripping it again. The weight of the wooden weapon was almost too much with my injured and weak right arm. I switched to my left. That didn't feel any better, but it wasn't any worse.

"Are you left-handed?" she asked.

"Both hands are equal for me."

She nodded and raised that left brow of hers once again. "Part two of the test: your turn, hit me."

I could be quick if I needed to be, but I didn't have any illusions that I was quicker than her.

I swung for her right hip.

Again, her movements were too quick for me to see. I just felt the results: another numb hand as the sword was torn away, another stinging shoulder and...

"Oh!" I gasped. She was right up in my face, her sword rubbing against my neck. The message was clear. I was dead.

"I take it I failed?" I said, a bit disheartened.

She stepped back, dropping the practice sword from my neck. "No."

I blinked. "But... I... I don't understand."

She spoke as she picked up my weapon. "I can teach speed and we can work on strength, but there is one thing I can't teach, and I wouldn't train you if you didn't have it." She looked at me directly. "Heart, courage."

Oh?

"You passed the moment you agreed to do the second test. You were in pain and could have run away, tail between your legs, but you didn't. You stood your ground, knowing it was going to hurt. That takes courage. I'll teach you." She grinned. "For one strip a session, in advance."

I shrugged, and regretted it instantly, given both of my injured shoulders. Reaching for the pouch at my belt I undid the clasp and pulled out five strips handing them over to her. "Here's the cost for today, plus the next four sessions. I figure we can reassess where I am at that point."

She hesitated, eyes a bit wide. It was clear she was not wealthy if five strips of silver impressed her. She took them reverently. "Agreed."

"Is there more to today's lesson, or just humiliation and pain?"

She laughed. "Did you want more? How do you feel? I pulled those hits, but still…"

Those had been *pulled*? That wasn't her full strength? *By Brovos!*

But I wanted to impress her. I wasn't sure why impressing this common woman was suddenly so important, but it was. "I'm good to continue," I said. "As long as I get armor too."

Another laugh from her, more of a guffaw, with a bit of a snort. "I like you. Yes, you can have some armor. I'm glad you're sticking with it. There may be more to you than a skinny nobleman. This way."

I didn't know why, but with her raucous laughter and her backhanded compliment about being 'more than a skinny nobleman,' she was growing on me. I think it was because no one had ever dared be that forthright with me in my life. More than that, Tisera was giving me exactly what I wanted and needed, a chance to learn combat. This woman fascinated me in a way no other ever had. A growing part of me wanted to be around her, impress her... even if I was going to get hurt...

... a lot.

CHAPTER 5

Dazar

I didn't recognize the man in the yard with Dizzy as I returned home from the university. He looked to be a nobleman, given the blond hair and jewel-toned eyes, and it appeared Dizzy was teaching him swordplay. Had she finally found a job? If so, I was happy for her. I knew how much it galled her that I'd had to help pay last month's taxes.

Dizzy and I nodded to each other in passing as I went into the house to change. After I passed them, I overheard:

"Is that a Phorasti?" came the man's voice.

"Yes," Dizzy replied. "My brother."

"Your brother is a—"

The door shut firmly behind me and I sighed. That was not an unusual reaction, and one reason I didn't like wearing my official Phorasti robes: too much attention and curiosity.

Then I sighed for a completely different reason: Dizzy had called me her brother.

And I was...

...sort of.

Her father had adopted me after the Dath-Riven War.

The trouble was, I didn't see her as a sister. She was the love of my life, but despite all my powers, I'd never had the courage to tell her. I didn't want to ruin the pleasant relationship we had. We lived together, even if it was in separate rooms. I saw her every day. We laughed and joked together. It was a good life.

But if I told her how I felt, and that wasn't what she wanted, everything would become awkward. I'd probably have to move out, which was the last thing I wanted.

I didn't know what to do.

For all that everyone gawked at my Phorasti powers, and the status that came with them, I was a coward when it came to the woman I loved.

Shoulders slumped, I went to my room and took off my Phorasti robes. As much as I hated them, they opened a lot of doors for me. Being the only Phorasti of any significant rank within the city of Pearlia, I was called upon *a lot*.

My trip this morning had not been planned. A runner had come from the university. One of the professors had fallen from a ladder in the library and needed healing. It had taken me some time to perform the delicate mending of bone and restitching of sinew and muscle. I was utterly exhausted, but also two gold royals richer.

Not that money mattered to me. I already had a small fortune and nothing to spend it on. Dizzy wouldn't let me help her with the finances for the cottage and grounds and I had few other needs so... I repaid her in small ways, using my powers to encourage the garden in the back, and giving gifts on her birthday and Festival Days — she wouldn't take gifts any other time, too much pride — but that was it.

I sat heavily on my bed in the darkness of my room. Though for me, it wasn't dark at all. Everything around me radiated an aura. This was the gift of the Phorasti, or more specifically a Kromasti, though few outside the White Tower would make that distinction. Every living thing had an aura and most of the furniture was made from once living materials and still held a trace of their aura.

The wood in the wardrobe, the desk, and the bed frame gave off a green hue. Even the cloth mattress and the feathers which stuffed it gave off faint hues of green and gold. The chunks of ash in the hearth, dark to any other, were simmering orange to my Phorasti senses.

I thought about laying down, but hearing the scuffing and sparring out in the yard next to my room did not seem conducive to rest, so I dressed in some rough clothes and went to encourage the garden.

I left the house and crossed the yard quickly, getting out of Dizzy's way, but paused once I was in the garden.

Even without looking I could feel Dizzy's aura. Mostly she was red, the color of passion and strength, it billowed off her like no one else, a heady cloud. I'd gotten used to it, but it had overwhelmed me often as a boy when I'd first been coming into my powers. Her aura also possessed heavy strokes of yellow for her courage and vitality. Lesser, but still noticeable, were traces of violet and purple for her wisdom and presence, and blue for her integrity and wit. It wasn't uncommon for people to give off many colors, but the sheer force of Dizzy's aura made me, well... dizzy. Everyone thought my nickname for her came from her dizzying combat ability and how fast she moved, and... it was. But for me it had a whole other meaning.

The aura of the noble with her was quite colorful and complex, but nowhere near as strong as Dizzy's. He possessed a base of strong blue, violet, and purple with undertones of gold, a hint of orange, and thin streamers of yellow and green. A very eclectic man indeed.

I sighed and knelt next to a patch of cabbage, feeling the greenness of its energy. I expanded my aura to connect with this small plant. If Dizzy's aura was strong enough to dazzle me, the aura of a full Phorasti like me would be overwhelming even to someone who wasn't sensitive to such things. It was one of the reasons why the first lesson any Phorasti was taught was how to restrain their aura until and unless needed. Even normal people, despite not being able to see our colors, would still feel and be affected by a strong aura, becoming dazed and addled. So, I had to keep my aura contained, most of the time.

I touched the cabbage's aura and felt for any disease or impurities, even if only traces, and weeded them out before moving on to the next. Shorine's garden had never been so lush and bountiful as it was since I'd returned to

Pearlia last year. I loved the simplicity of working with these plants. They were nowhere near as complex as people.

People could be harsh and violent and... with the sparring not that far away behind me, my mind pulled me back to memories of the war...

I could see it vividly, my senses alive with the stench and sounds of that final — *horrible* — battle for Vestrea City. The Pearlian forces defended, under siege. The Eromorn army swarmed like ants — in the thousands — around the walls. The city had been under siege for months, our forces dwindling, out of food, and desperate.

I'd been called to help lift the siege.

My jaw tightened, as it had that day... when I'd done what had been commanded of me. I'd never used my powers to harm anyone before that day, nor since. I'd killed enough men that day for a dozen lifetimes. It had been far too easy, pulling their colors to me, sapping their life energies. Between one heartbeat and the next, more than three thousand men had drawn their last breath and fallen still.

I returned to myself as the memory faded, eyes clenched shut, tears leaking from them as I shuddered violently. I hoped Dizzy was distracted with her instruction and didn't see me shaking. She didn't know what I'd done.

What I'd done... to save her.

For she'd been one of the many Pearlian soldiers trapped in the city. That had been the *only* reason I'd even considered doing what I'd done. To free her. And she could never know. If she did, she'd turn from me in disgust, as any rational person would. I could never forgive myself for what I'd done, so how could she?

"Daz?"

The soft voice — not Dizzy's — startled me, even though I'd sensed someone coming. I didn't have to look to know it was Avela. Not only did I know her voice well, but I felt her colors. She was mostly orange and yellow with layers of lime and green, and various threads of red, sienna, blue, violet, even black. Black wasn't common for most people. Avela, however had dark secrets from her past, which had left their mark upon her spirit.

Dizzy and I knew some of her story, that she'd worked for a brothel for a time before catching the waning sickness and being tossed out into the street. That had been where Shorine had found her. The elderly shepherdess had brought Avela here and had nursed her back to health. We didn't need to know details, but it was clear she'd had a harsh life before she'd come to live with us.

"Are you well?" she asked with concern.

"I am," I said, forcing my voice to be strong. "It's been a tiring day, though."

"Take a break then. Come, have some cool water from the well. Sit with me in the shade and rest."

That sounded wonderful. I quickly shifted my colors and dried the few tears I'd shed. I stood and followed her down the path to the shaded trees on the other side of the juniper grove. There we sat and she drew some water from a bucket into small cups for us.

It was easy to talk to Avela. I had no attachments to her. I could be myself. Though, I did feel her reds and siennas swell. She liked me, was attracted to me. I was flattered, but I tried not to encourage such things. My heart belonged to Dizzy.

When she put her hand on my leg, I removed it gently.

She sighed and her reds and siennas faded. "You... should tell her how you feel," she said softly.

I nodded. Avela was perceptive, I wasn't surprised she knew how I felt about Dizzy. I just wish Dizzy knew.

"I know. I just don't know how."

"Just... say it." She rose from the bench we'd been sitting on and knelt before me taking my hand. Her voice grew soft and solemn. "I love you," she said... and she meant it. That *she* — Avela — loved *me*. Then she released my hand and rose quickly a pleasant smile on her face, the seriousness gone and her true feelings hidden. "Like that."

"Easy for you, but—"

"No Daz," she said, the seriousness returning. "That wasn't easy at all." She turned away, heading for the small caretaker's house next to the barn. Her aura shifted to muddled browns and the aching black of sorrow and confused sadness.

I sighed. I hadn't been thinking. Of course it hadn't been easy for her to say she loved me when she knew I didn't love her in return.

I'd messed up.

I hadn't considered her feelings. Here I was, with so much power, but I still had no clue how to talk to people. That was one of the reasons I didn't want to tell Dizzy any of this. What if I said the wrong thing?

What if I drove her away?

The other reason was, even assuming I said every-thing right... if Dizzy didn't feel the same way, then I'd feel as dejected and devastated as Avela had been just now.

I sighed again. Today was not going well at all.

The voices and sounds of occasional combat in the yard had stopped. I couldn't see the yard from this bench, so I rose and made my way along beside the garden, down the path back to the cottage.

The yard was empty.

I paused before I opened the door to the cottage, feeling Dizzy approaching from the other side, her aura like a soothing balm around me as it encompassed me.

The door opened and there she was... wrapped in a towel and nothing more.

"Oh! Daz! I was going to have a bath."

Yes, that was obvious.

"Care to join me?"

Not going to happen.

I stammered.

"At least come warm the water for me." She grabbed my hand and drew me along behind her as I tried not to look at... her.

She must have noticed. "Oh, come on Daz. It's not like we didn't bathe together as kids. You've seen me naked enough times."

True, but naked as a kid and naked as an adult were two *very* different things. Lots of kids ran around naked, not so many adults did.

I had to work very hard — especially with how tired I

was — to calm my reds and siennas so I didn't get an unsightly bulge in my pants.

Once we were through the door of the bathing area, she heaved me toward the bath and I did as she'd asked. I drew forth orange, warming the waters, my hand in the bath to test it.

I ignored how Dizzy sat on the edge of the tub, her slender ankles and the heavy round muscles of her calves in the water.

"Ooooh, yes, that's great, thanks." She stood, removing her towel, putting it on the rim, and stepped down into the waters. I looked down at the water, not up at her, but I still caught her reflection. A perfect woman, strong and powerful, lithe and graceful.

This time I couldn't stop my arousal from surging, my cock swelling, but painfully restrained.

"You look like you could use a soak." I could hear the concern in her voice. And I *could* use a soak, but not with her, not like this. She'd see how I felt for her clearly enough.

Wouldn't that just be the most awkward way to tell her? *"Hey Dizzy, yeah, I love you and get rock hard when I think of you. Wanna fuck in the bath?"*

I turned and left, not another word. I could hardly even breathe until I'd closed the door of the bathing area behind me. I heard Dizzy's bewildered, "Daz?"

I fell to my knees, addled and disoriented. I shouldn't have imagined that scenario of possibly joining her. Now I couldn't get it out of my head and my body responded viscerally to those vivid thoughts.

I stood awkwardly and staggered back to the house,

shutting myself in my room. Once alone, I freed my cock and stroked it hard. I pictured us in the bath together, her straddling me, taking me hard, demanding her pleasure and receiving it. Her hands rose up into her hair as she came, crying out. My hands caressed her high breasts, adding to her bliss. Then...

I grunted as my release came.

I emptied myself onto the cold ash of the hearth, leaning on the small mantle. And when I was done, I brought forth flames to scour the area clean.

I gulped air, confused and aroused and... alone.

Falling onto my bed, I berated myself for my continued cowardice.

I could be with the woman I loved, if I just told her how I felt. But... if she didn't feel the same, I'd feel far worse than I did now.

So, I traded an imagined pain for a very real one, and tried not to dream of what life would be like if Dizzy and I were truly together. For that was the most exquisite pain of all.

CHAPTER 6

Tɪsᴇʀᴀ

I ʜᴏᴘᴇᴅ Dᴀᴢ ᴡᴀꜱ ᴡᴇʟʟ. Hᴇ'ᴅ ꜱᴇᴇᴍᴇᴅ... ᴏꜰꜰ.

Though, he was always a bit awkward around me. Apparently, even powerful Phorasti mystics didn't know how to deal with aberrant warrior-women.

I sighed.

Or maybe this was just Daz being Daz. He was far too up tight most of the time. He'd been an awkward kid and turned into an awkward adult.

He probably just needed to get laid. He and Avela were together often enough that I suspected there was more than just a casual friendship between them. He certainly didn't seem awkward around her, which wasn't a surprise since she was gorgeous. Still, I didn't think he'd slept with her yet. Perhaps, after my bath, I'd go and tell him to bed the woman, for Halea's sake! Maybe that would help him loosen up?

I sighed and relaxed into the warm waters.

It had been a strange — but very lucrative — day. Leo had given me a tidy sum and tomorrow I'd get a small fortune from Prince Victor. And all I had to do was babysit a noblewoman and train a nobleman not to be a mess with a sword. I smiled and slid down into the warm waters until they covered my neck and chin.

Leo was quick and had the potential to be a decent dualist-type swordsman. He'd need to bulk up *a lot* more to ever wield a heavy-blade well but put a rapier or side-sword in his hand and he might just be a threat... eventually.

And by the gods he was handsome!

I wasn't usually one for the noble look of blond hair and jewel-tone eyes, but Leo was far more than the sum of those parts. He was... beautiful.

Before today, I hadn't thought I'd like a beautiful man. I usually went for the big and rugged type with a strong jaw and weathered face, like Kel, who I didn't want to think about right now.

Apparently, I had more expansive tastes. Perhaps it was the subtle dimple on Leo's chin, or the high sharp cheeks? I didn't know for certain. And as much as he was tall and lanky, he had some muscle on that frame of his, it just wasn't trained for combat... yet.

But his muscle might be trained... for loving?

The question was: would he want a strange, strong woman like me? Though, as I thought about that, something occurred to me. Leo hadn't been intimidated by me, like most men.

Once we'd had a chance to talk and work together,

he'd seemed easy going — even friendly — around me. That, plus his gorgeous looks, meant he was the best candidate for a fling I'd had in a while. Halea knew how much I needed a fuck. I hadn't had a cock in my nethers since the war! And I didn't know if Leo would be up for showing me his *other* sword, but I was very much looking forward to seeing him again.

Because as much as I — like Daz — needed to get laid, I couldn't bring myself to visit the brothels of the city, even if the men there were said to be exquisite in their ability to please a woman. And I didn't have the energy to go out looking for a man who wasn't intimidated by me. I figured the right one would find me some day.

And I didn't know if Leo was right, but he was the only candidate to have come around in a while.

So, I closed my eyes and imagined those long, slender fingers of his tracing over my body. He caressed my face and ran his hand up into my hair as he pulled me close for a kiss. His lips were soft and yielding, but his tongue could dance like a courtier. His other hand moved over the side of my breast, his thumb sneaking in to circle my nipple, slowly rousing the flesh to a taut peak. Then that same hand slid down my side and between my legs. His long fingers played in my slick folds, nimbly stroking my clit until I was a moaning, quivering mess.

Then he lifted me and...

Lifted me?

Could he lift me? I was a sturdy woman with solid muscle, which meant I wasn't light. I could probably lift him, but that wouldn't do either of us any good.

My imaginings broke apart.

I sighed as the day-dream faded. I'd have to pleasure myself for the time being... and a warm bath was just the place to do it.

I felt loose and relaxed when I finally got out of the tepid waters.

I hadn't had a midday meal yet and from the angle of the sun, it was long past time. I expected to be greeted inside with a meal, since Daz usually liked — and was very good at — such domestic duties. But there was no food prepared and Daz was nowhere to be seen. The door to his room closed.

I sighed, not wanting to interrupt whatever he might be doing — probably some important Phorasti things — and found some dried meat and a few pieces of fruit, taking those to my room.

I'd have to send Avela out to pick up some special items to eat, to celebrate my newfound success and income.

But once I'd eaten, I was so relaxed I fell asleep on my bed, half-clothed. I woke hungry late in the evening, but again no evening meal had been prepared. Whatever Daz was doing, it must be important and lengthy.

I grabbed a bit more of the dried meat and fruit for my meal and returned to my bed. Tomorrow, I'd escort Veora to the market... perhaps I'd buy something interesting for my celebratory meal. I fell asleep dreaming of foods I'd never had and a man with green eyes ravishing me.

I did indeed pick up some exotic foods from the New Market the next day while out with Veora. My usual indulgence of choice was oranges. They were a local fruit, but very expensive and usually reserved for nobles.

Also, a caravan had come in from the south with many other exotic things to taste. Veora was far more knowledgeable than I on these delicacies and counselled me on what to try. There were kaffa beans, which could be ground up and put in water to make a hot drink of some sort. I had some ground at the market to try at home. She also introduced me to Jhokala, an odd, hard, black bar, which had an extremely bitter flavor, but apparently if combined with something sweet could be quite tasty. We tried a few shavings on orange slices and the Jhokala's rich flavor, mixed very well with the sweetness of the orange. I picked up a bar to experiment with. I also picked up a bag of mixed nuts from the south-west which included: pecans, almonds, and cashews, none of which I'd tried before, but Veora assured me they were quite tasty.

Veora picked up two fruits called avocados and tomatoes. I was unfamiliar with these — both were from the south — but when I tried them, I was instantly hooked. The last new wonder I discovered was a large, green, striped melon with the uninspiring name of watermelon. But it was far sweeter than the name suggested, and I took one home as well.

I also purchased a few dresses. If I was going to look the part of a "friend" of Veora's and not her guard, then I'd need some new clothes. Most of what I owned were pants and shirts — men's clothes — and not very womanly. So, I found a few dresses in which I'd be able to move around well.

Veora was bubbly and chatty, which I usually found annoying, but something about her drew me in. She was easy to be around and welcoming. Perhaps it wouldn't be so bad escorting her hither and yon for a while.

I returned home with my haul of treasures, hopeful and excited to see what Daz might be able to whip up with them. But he wasn't there. Avela said he'd gone out but hadn't told her where. So, my dinner wasn't particularly inspired in how it was prepared, but it was still delicious.

The next day, Daz was late to get up. I began wondering if he was avoiding me for some reason. He was usually quite happy to do all things domestic for me. After my morning calisthenics I saw him working in the garden and went to him.

"Hey, you doing well?" I asked. "You've been in your room or away a lot the last day or so. I was starting to worry."

He didn't look up from the garden as he said: "Oh... ah, hey Dizzy. Yeah, I'm well, just... busy, that's all."

I guessed that was to be expected as one of the few Phorasti in the city. My mind turned to all the delicacies I'd picked up yesterday. Excited, I asked, "Did you see the haul of exotic foods I picked up?"

He looked up at me and smiled, though he still seemed distracted. "Ah... what? Oh... yes, I did."

When he didn't elaborate, I asked, "Do you think you could make something special for dinner tonight? I have two new jobs and I'd like to celebrate!"

"Oh! That's great, Dizzy!" His smile deepened,

caramel brown eyes sparkling. "I'm happy for you. Yeah, I'll see what I can do." He rose, dusting off his hands.

"You're amazing! Thanks," I said, grinning ear to ear. I drew him into a tight hug and, after a moment he seemed to relax and return the gesture.

He seemed well enough. I wasn't sure why I'd been worried. He hadn't been avoiding me. He was just an important and busy man.

"Whatever you need, I'm... here for you," he whispered, head beside mine, pulling me just a little tighter into the embrace.

I sighed. Everything was right with the world again. "I know," I said. "I'm here for you too. That's what family is for."

CHAPTER 7

TISERA

THAT AFTERNOON, I PUT ON ONE OF MY NEW DRESSES. IT was dark orange-red, with long flaring skirts which ended mid-calf. It had good leg mobility and enough skirt to easily hide a long dagger strapped upside-down to each thigh. It showed a lot more of my chest than I was comfortable with, but that was the style of the day, a square-cut neckline, low enough to show the tops of my breasts.

Oh well.

Daz caught sight of me as I left and stared, stunned.

I grimaced. "Is it that bad? I know I don't wear a lot of dresses, but—"

"No," he whispered. "It's... perfect, you're perfect. You're beautiful."

I may have blushed then. Though perhaps as my brother, he had to say things like that.

"Thanks, Daz." I slapped him on the shoulder and he seemed to snap out of his reverie.

"Ah... don't get me wrong," he stammered. "You've always been perfect and beautiful."

Yeah, *that* was too much, definitely something a brother had to say. Still, it was nice to hear. I laughed, feeling just a bit lighter as I left.

The walk to Veora's house gave me time to get a feel for the new garments. The wide skirt gave full range of motion with my legs and the half-sleeve meant nearly full range of motion with my arms, though I was certain I'd tear the shoulders if I did anything too rough in it.

When Veora came out to meet me, she seemed a bit surprised and looked me over quickly. She smiled and laughed when she saw my feet. "We need to work on your footwear," she said softly. "Most women don't wear heavy boots like that."

I blinked.

My boots?

She wore sandals with souls of thick leather tied over light slippers. That was quite different from my tight, military-style boots, which came up to mid-calf. But I honestly wasn't sure how I'd fare in footwear like hers.

"We'll see," I said skeptically. "I'm already feeling out of place in a dress. One step at a time."

She laughed at that and nodded. She wore another pink dress, this one darker in shade than the last, edging on purple. Her neckline was even lower than mine and showed off her ample bust. Again, I didn't know if she was wearing a corset or not, but I was beginning to think not. She just had an ideal figure.

She looped her arm in mine, humming a pleasant tune before saying: "Come friend, let's walk."

We were about halfway to the city gate when she stopped her humming — it was a near constant thing for her — and spoke again.

"Well, if we are to be fast friends, then we must learn more about each other. I'll go first. Ask me anything you'd like."

It wasn't politic at all, but the thing I was most curious about was: "Why are you with Prince Victor?"

She coughed a little, probably at the bluntness of my question. "You get right to it, don't you? Ah... well..." She sighed. "That was not my choice, at least at first."

"No?" That was curious. "Did he force himself on you?"

"No," she said with a hint of hesitation. "Not quite, but when the prince of the realm asks you to dance you don't refuse. We met at a ball a few months back."

Her tone turned nostalgic, wistful. "My family's estate is far to the west. My brother and I lived there, with our mother, while my father — who was quite a bit older than my mother — lived here at the estate near the city so he could be available for any session of the Nobles' court."

Sadness tinged her words. "But my father passed last winter and my brother came to take his place. I came to see the city as well. And during my first foray into society, the crown prince came to me and swept me up in a dance and..." she trailed off.

"And?"

Veora spoke slowly, a strange mix of desire and

tension in her voice. "And... after that dance, he took me out into a servants' hall. We were both flushed from the swift pace of the dance and... he kissed me. He wasn't forceful about it, and I didn't mind it, but I did wonder about his wife. I'd thought him happily married, but when I asked, he said his wife had not come to his bed in some time and when he'd seen me..."

She leaned close and lowered her voice. "He said that when he saw me, he'd known instantly that he'd never truly loved his wife. Theirs had been a political marriage and he'd been well with that, until he'd seen me. When he did, he said his heart had leaped like a dancer. Only then did he know what true love was."

"Oh," I said, just a bit stunned.

"Indeed. I was flattered and he is a very handsome man and... well... our kissing quickly became *more*. After he'd taken me, right there in the servants' hall, he said this one encounter would never be enough. He said he had to see me again."

"And you agreed?" I still didn't quite understand this.

Her tone became neutral with just a hint of an edge to it. "He is the crown prince. How did you feel when he asked you to do this for him? Did you feel like you could deny him?"

"No. I see."

"Exactly." Her tone eased and she smiled. "And... to be fair, I was beginning to feel something for him too. He is handsome and gallant and—" her breath became a whisper, "—quite an amazing lover."

She sighed again. "I was a bit afraid of what would

happen if I said no, but a part of me didn't *want* to say no, so... here we are."

I grunted. It wasn't a very womanly thing to do, and Veora laughed a little. Yet her mirth quickly turned somber.

She whispered when she said: "I am a bit... ashamed at what our relationship is doing to his family. His wife is even more distant now. Some part of me still thinks I should end this with Victor, so he can be with his family. But... he doesn't seem to care. And in all honestly, when I'm with him, neither do I. When he touches me, when he kisses me, I suddenly feel like we're the only two people in the world."

She grimaced. "I know it's not right, but I *do* love him, and I know he loves me. My mind says I should go, but my heart doesn't want to."

"It seems a difficult position he's put you in."

"No, it's not like that. I mean, yes, at first, it was quite awkward, but now... now there is only our love. And I'll take that for as long as he'll give it. I have no illusions that this will end someday. The Queen is already furious with him."

Veora gazed off at the city wall above us as we neared the gate. "Someday he'll realize he can't truly have me, and that will be that. I'll treasure the time we had together and I'll... find another man... assuming any man will have a woman as... *well known* as I am."

I nodded.

We walked in silence for a while before she said. "Now your turn. Tell me something about yourself, anything!"

Perhaps her talk of love and relationships had gotten into my head, but the only thing I could think to talk about was Leo. So, as we walked, I told her of the man and how beautiful he was.

"He's captured your heart, like the prince captured mine," she said softly. "What will you do about it?"

What *would* I do?

She prompted: "If he asks to court you, or perhaps just to... to bed you... would you accept?"

That was easy.

"Courting seems unlikely. A nobleman would never formally court a commoner like me. But if he wanted to dally, I'd be more than happy to oblige him."

I'd spent far too much time over the last few days wondering what Leo would be like in bed. I'd only ever slept with military men, who were rough and ready. And I liked that... a lot. But I had a feeling Leo wouldn't be like that. I imagined he'd be soft and sensuous. I had no clue what that was like, but a part of me desperately wanted to know.

Veora giggled. "You'd rather bed him than court him? Most women would have it the other way around. You're a strange one, Tisi. Not like any other woman I know."

That was very true.

CHAPTER 8

TISERA

WE CHATTED UNTIL WE REACHED THE PALACE. THEN WE began the first run through of our clandestine process for getting to Prince Victor's rooms.

The guards at the servant's gate had been told to expect us and ushered us through. We passed through a storeroom and some kitchens before slipping into the servant's halls. Once we reached the royal wing of the palace, we entered secret hallways, which even the servants didn't know about. Those brought us out close to the prince's rooms, only a short walk out in the open.

Before we returned to the regular halls, I checked to make sure the way was clear before escorting Veora to the prince's chambers.

After I'd handed Veora over to the prince, I asked if I could go see my aunt, while I was there. Since I was already in the royal wing it wouldn't be that far to

Princess Alice's suite. Victor agreed, telling me to return at the fourth bell. I left the lovers and made my way to Princess Alice's suite.

Luckily, it was my aunt who answered my knock on the door and greeted me warmly.

"Who is it?" came the light and breathy voice of Princess Alice from deeper inside the suite.

"My niece Tisera," Aunt Emri called back and closed the door behind me. We made our way through the entrance hall to the main room where Princess Alice struggled to stand. Emri went and helped her up.

Alice had been weak and frail ever since she'd contracted the waning sickness as a child. She'd survived, but had been sickly ever since, even as a grown woman. She was a few years older than I, but quite small and slight of build, very fragile. She had the same blond hair and jewel eyes of all royals and most nobility. In her case, the hair was more a flaxen tone, a bit washed out, and the eyes a very pale blue.

"Come, sister," she said, arms open.

It was what she called me whenever I came to visit my aunt. I'd grown to know and love this small princess, and since Emri had been like a mother to both of us, Alice always referred to me as her sister.

It warmed my heart.

I went to her and embraced her, very carefully. She was so weak I almost didn't feel her hug. And even that much effort tired her. She swooned, unsteady on her feet. I helped her back to her chair, where Emri laid a blanket over her lap.

"Too much excitement!" she breathed, yet she smiled

wide. "But I do love a visit." Her face clouded a little after that.

I sat in the chair next to hers, pulling it close and held out a hand for her to clasp.

I felt sorry for the woman. Even though she was a royal, she was pretty much confined to these rooms, partly because she didn't have the stamina to go far beyond them, and partly on orders from the queen.

Alice had always been the black sheep of the family because of her frailty. The other royals tended to avoid her, not wanting to be reminded of what might have happened to them, if they'd been unlucky enough to have caught the same illness.

Alice was a stain on the otherwise active and hearty family. As such, I was one of her few visitors. Though, Prince Leonin did stop by now and then, of all her siblings he was the most welcoming of her. Thinking of Leonin, brought to mind Leo, the nobleman I'd started training, and I must have flushed a little.

Alice noticed. "Oh! Tisi, what is it? Are you well?" Alice asked.

Emri sat nearby in another chair, listening intently. She was a bit more worldly and very perceptive.

"No, I believe your mention of a visit got my niece thinking of someone visiting her. Is that right? A man perhaps?" my aunt said with a knowing smile. She seemed happy that I might have finally found a suitor.

"Yes," I breathed and laughed.

"Oh, Tisi! That's wonderful, who is he?" Alice asked, squeezing my hand, with little strength in the gesture.

"His name is Leo. One of the many nobles named after your brother."

"Yes," Alice laughed. "There was an abundance of Leos after my brother was named. It seemed to catch on amongst the nobility."

"Well, one of them found me," I said.

"A noble?" my aunt asked, very curious and excited.

"Yes, but... he's not interested in me in the way you think, at least, not yet. He came to me for combat lessons, practice with a sword. I don't know why he came to me when many others in the city could train him. Yet he seems glad I took him on and he's paying me well."

"And is he handsome?" Alice asked, flushing a little. She'd never married. No man had even been allowed to court her. Her mother had forbidden it. Such... excitement... would be too much for her. And in truth, it might be. Certainly, the trials of childbirth would have been brutal, if not fatal for Alice. But still, she'd been denied so much, so she had to live vicariously through others.

"Not handsome," I said finding myself blushing a little more. "But *beautiful*, with delicate features and soft, caring eyes." I wasn't sure where that description had come from. It was true, but I wouldn't usually have described anyone that way.

"Oh, you *have* fallen for him, haven't you?" Emri said with a laugh.

"You certainly speak of him as a lover might," Alice added.

I laughed. This was all so new for me. I drew a long breath to calm myself.

"Perhaps, but I have no clue if he feels the same, and

even if he did, the chances of a relationship would be slim. He's a noble and I'm not. We might... have a little fun, but it could never go farther than that."

"Trust me, girl, have some fun if you get the chance. Love, or even just the passing affections of something like this are... rare." My aunt ended with a sigh. She spoke from experience.

She'd never married.

I'd gone to live with her when she was just sixteen. And having a baby in her life — even one that wasn't her own — had made it very difficult for her to find a man to court her. She'd never complained about it, and it had turned out to be a boon when she'd been selected to be Princess Alice's lady's maid, since the position was for an unwed woman.

Still...

I nodded to her. Perhaps I would ask Leo if he'd like... *something else.* Or perhaps he might ask me first? I didn't think it likely, but I could hope.

"What brings you to the palace?" Alice asked and I was caught a little off guard. I should have expected a question like this. I couldn't tell them I was bringing Prince Victor's mistress.

"I... just wanted to see you both. It's been so long," I lied. It *had* been too long. I should have come to see them on my own without having had any other reason to come, which meant I now felt horrible.

"It has," Alice said with a smile. "I'm glad you came." She sighed. "As you might have noticed, today's been a rough day."

At times, it was almost impossible to tell Alice was

afflicted. Some days she felt well enough to walk in the palace gardens, though no farther than that. Today she seemed particularly weak.

Alice looked out the many windows streaming sunlight into her rooms. "Sometimes I think that we are connected, Tisi," she said a bit dreamily. "Two parts of some whole. The world made me weak so you could be strong, as strong as a man, perhaps stronger." She smiled, though it was tinged with sadness.

"I... I never knew..." I said softly. It was an interesting compliment, if a horrible thought. I certainly hoped that I hadn't taken strength from another to become who I was. "If I could give you my strength..." I would help her if I could.

She turned to me, the sad smile growing bright. "You *do* give me strength Tisi. That's the other reason I have this strange fantasy, because every time you're here I always feel stronger." She squeezed my hand again and oddly... it *was* more forceful.

"I'm... touched," I said. "I'm glad my visits help."

"They do," my aunt said softly. "Very much." I sensed a subtle admonition in those words. I shouldn't be a stranger.

"I'll come more often," I vowed. Certainly, I'd be here at the palace much more often now, with Veora's visits. "It's a promise."

"I'm so glad," Alice said. "Now." She perked up, definitely livelier than when I'd arrived. "What else is new in your life Tisi? You must tell us everything!"

So, I did. Though there wasn't much new to tell. I didn't feel comfortable mentioning Prince Victor, at least not yet, so not much else in my life had changed. Yet, when conversation turned from me to life at the palace, Prince Victor quickly came up. Alice was conspicuously silent, but my aunt had a lot to say:

"I can't believe that man! He seemed perfectly respectable and reasonable, then suddenly he's pushing his wife and family away and seeing this hussy! I don't know who to blame: this new noblewoman, whoever she is, or Prince Victor himself for being so weak willed and lustful as to pursue her! It's shameful. The man should be flogged for his infidelity. It makes me glad I never married. Men can be so... ugh! Just... like... *Men!*"

I couldn't fault that logic. Certainly, the one man I'd thought I'd loved had broken my heart, leaving me after the war with only the words: "I'll be back!" But Kel had never come back. He'd returned to Pearlia and apparently forgotten about me.

We continued to chat until the fourth bell, when I made my way back to Prince Victor's rooms. Veora was flushed and a little disheveled, but she hid it well.

I walked her back to her house, then returned home.

When I arrived, Daz was there with an odd look on his face.

"You'd said you'd gotten a couple of new jobs, but I'd never expected..." He motioned to a small chest on the table. "Someone came by while you were out and dropped that off. There are twenty-four strips of silver in it! They said it was three months' payment. What job did you get: guarding a prince?"

Close.

"Not quite." I smiled at the look of wonder on his soft

brown features. "Let me get changed out of this damned dress, then I'll tell you all about it."

I was halfway to my room, with one of the ties on the dress already undone when Daz called to me. "No! Ah... wait... Leave the dress on."

I turned back with a questioning glance, one brow raised.

He smiled. "A celebratory meal deserves a special dress, doesn't it?"

I cocked my head. He wasn't wrong. "And what will you wear?" I asked.

He blinked. "Ah... well... I've got some nice things I could put on."

"Are they comfortable?" I asked. Because this dress wasn't: not with the way the ties sinched tightly around my waist and under my bust and the restrictive shoulders, not to mention the draft up my legs.

"Well... no... but..."

"Deal," I said. "I'll wear this uncomfortable thing, if you wear your most uncomfortable thing, and we'll both be uncomfortable together eating a special dinner."

He grinned, then laughed. "Deal."

I liked it when Daz laughed, so light and free, a truly joyous sound, which filled me with warmth. Yet he did it so rarely. He was too serious and up tight.

He changed, returning in a tightly-fitted suit, which accentuated his strong shoulders and arms, taut over his rolling muscles. The entire ensemble was black, a buttoned shirt under the snug coat, and well-trimmed pants falling perfectly to just above his booted feet.

"Very dashing!" I said, hoping that was the appropriate sisterly comment. His words from this morning about my dress still sat uneasy with me.

He smiled, and even blushed a little, before returning to the cooking area to gather the meal he'd made.

I sat at the table, watching as he brought the various dishes over. "So, what have you cooked up for me?"

He laughed again. "I don't know if it's worth twenty-four strips of silver, but I've done what I could with the wide variety of foods you bought."

Oh, right, I'd been going to tell him about my new jobs. So, as he finished bringing the last couple items to the table, I told him about my work for the prince and that it was highly sensitive and not to tell anyone. He already knew about Leo, but I mentioned that his lessons might continue for a while as well.

"Then you have certainly earned this meal," he said, dishing out the dinner he'd made onto two plates. "I hope you enjoy it."

And I did, very much. The mix of flavors, some strong, some delicate, was perfect. The textures and tastes danced on my tongue and filled me with such delight I actually moaned and sighed my way through the various bites.

"This is almost better than sex!" I said around a mouthful, savoring it. I'd never had an orgasm from food before, but this came very close.

Daz blushed again, dark red staining his soft brown cheeks. "Ah... thanks?" he said softly.

He always got so flustered at talk of sex.

Oh! That reminded me. "You need to tell Avela how

you feel and get that woman into bed," I said as I reached for some wine.

He gaped at me.

I shook my head. Sometimes I wondered if the man was a virgin. He always got so fidgety and awkward whenever I mentioned sex.

"If you haven't been with a woman before, I could tell you some things she'd like." Though I wasn't like most women, so perhaps I shouldn't give advice. "Avela probably doesn't like it as rough as I do, so maybe not. But definitely, make sure to use your—"

"Dizzy, no!" His voice rose a few octaves as he cut me off, eyes wide. "No... I... you..." His lips moved with no sound before he found his words. "Avela and I are just friends, nothing more. I'd never think of bedding her. She's... she's not my type." He drew in a long breath. "Actually—"

"Then take some of this silver and buy yourself a top-notch whore," I suggested. "Pick out a pretty girl you like and wet your whistle with her."

He blanched. "Dizzy, no... I..."

I laughed at his awkward stammering. True, I wasn't one for whores either, but he really needed to get laid. And being the vicious sister I was, I couldn't help but goad him a bit more.

"If you're shy, I'm sure she'd teach you a thing or two. Actually, your birthday is coming up, isn't it? Maybe I'll buy one for you. Some round wench, all oiled up and ready for love. You're always getting me nice things, it's time I returned the favor."

It had been a joke, but the way Daz looked at me,

gaping, mouth bobbing open and closed, like a fish, he thought I was serious.

Still, he looked so silly I had to laugh. I couldn't figure out why he was so shocked by this. Though, if he was a virgin, then perhaps this was all a bit too much for him. Or, if he wasn't interested in Avela or other women, then...

"Or... do you like men?" In truth I didn't know what he liked. He'd never spoken of his affections at all. "No worries, I could get you a man if you like? A hard, handsome bloke, oiled up and ready for love. Or maybe one of each if you don't know which you want yet?"

Daz choked on nothing, coughing and sputtering.

I laughed harder, then sighed.

I didn't know what I could do to help the man lighten up. He seemed insistent on remaining clammed up, highstrung, and celibate. Though, to be fair, I hadn't had sex in a while either, but that's because I was picky.

Perhaps he was picky too?

Daz got up and walked out, still coughing and sputtering and bright red in the face. I'd teased him too much.

Still, he'd have to get laid someday. I just hoped he'd find the right partner soon and loosen up a bit.

Shaking my head, I went back to the glorious meal he'd made, feeling just the tiniest bit guilty about what I'd said. I shouldn't tease him so much... but then... he shouldn't make it so fun!

CHAPTER 9

TISERA

"NO, YOU'RE BEING TOO RIGID, USE MORE WRIST!" I HAD TO keep myself from yelling. "This is a much lighter weapon and needs finesse!"

I was halfway through my second training session with Leo but things were not going well. I'd been trying to teach him how to use a side-sword, but he'd been trained with an arming-sword and his stance and style were all wrong.

"No wonder you feel like you don't know what you're doing. Whoever tried to teach you didn't know the right weapon for you at all!" I sighed. "Just... forget everything you know and listen to me," I said gently.

Leo, sweaty and frustrated, nodded.

We were on my long front lawn, not far from the cottage. If one was going to fall on one's ass, this was a much softer place to do it than the packed earth of the yard. The lush grasses and softer soil here would add a bit of a cushion. We were both in a padded gambeson — I'd loaned him one of mine — and I could tell even just this slight added weight on the slender man fatigued him. He really needed to exercise more.

"Come on, sit down and rest," I said, sitting, crossing my legs.

He followed suit.

"I'm sorry, Miss Tisera," Leo said a little abashed and forlorn. "My trainers assumed I'd grow stronger and get used to the heavier weapons, like my brothers did." He sighed.

"If they'd had half a brain, they would have trained you in many weapons to see what you were best with. And if they were going to make you use an arming sword, they should have worked you up to it with smaller or lighter versions first. You might have fared much better. As it is now, you'll have to unlearn what you know to even *begin* with this weapon."

I blew out a breath, trying to figure out where to start. He'd need greater stamina to survive any fight, where one's strength could drain away quickly if one was too tense. Which also meant he needed to feel ready and able to face a fight, but that would only come with time and practice. Perhaps I shouldn't even have started him with a sword. Perhaps just hand-fighting would be a better place to start.

I liked that option.

"I have an idea. Come on, stand up and take off your armor." I did so first and threw the gambeson to one side.

He followed suit. The clothes beneath his armor —

he'd come more adequately attired this time, in a lose shirt and pants — were sodden with sweat and clinging to his lean frame. He might not be big, but he did have muscles. I could see them now, the tight, high muscles of a young, lean body. They just weren't developed for fighting.

I tried not to admire them too much, tearing my gaze off his tall form and getting back to business.

"We're going to start with the *real* basics: stance, movement, observing your enemy. And all of that can be done while hand-fighting. Have you ever thrown a punch?"

He grimaced. "Some families may have siblings who roughhouse a little, but mine... did not. No, I have never punched anyone or anything."

"Do you know how to make a fist?"

He did so and held it up. At least the thumb was on the outside, which was good.

"Good. Now what you want to do is have your arms up and ready. Most attacks will probably be aimed for your face or torso, so you need to keep your hands up to be able to block them."

I demonstrated.

He mimicked well, even adjusting his feet to match mine... almost.

"You're a little flat-footed, keep yourself up on the balls of your feet, knees bent, so you can move around on the spot a bit easier." I swayed a little. He watched, then did as I'd done.

"Good!" He was a quick learner.

He smiled.

I moved over to him and took one of his hands. "When you hit, you want to hit here." I put my hand to his fist indicating the flat part of the first two knuckles. "Otherwise, you might break some fingers." I put my hand up. "Try it, lightly."

He shifted, pushing his fist into my hand. I nodded. "That's it. Now, we'll try some basic punches and evasions." I spent the rest of the afternoon running him through his paces. He was quite adept and mastered the few things I showed him.

"No one has ever made things this easy to understand," he said as he ran through a series of moves, able to do it faster and faster every time he tried.

I smiled at his compliment.

"I bet there are women in the city who would love to know how to protect themselves. You could start a school, teaching women to fight."

I didn't think that likely.

Women wanted to be womanly... didn't they? They didn't want to be difficult and violent, like I was. Once they were able to fight, wouldn't that mean men in general would be intimidated by them... like me?

"I don't know," I said shaking my head. "I don't think many women want to be so... aggressive."

"You'd be surprised," Leo continued, confident.

I shrugged. "If you can find some women, I'll give it a try."

"I might take you up on that."

I grinned. I wouldn't mind the extra business, even if it didn't seem likely Leo would find anyone willing to participate.

"Well, how am I doing?" he asked.

Quite well, even if he was a bedraggled and sweaty mess. And something about this beautiful man shadow-boxing was turning me on something fierce. But that wasn't what he meant.

"You've mastered those moves. Next time I'll teach you some more. It's going to take a while, but we'll move you through more and more advanced unarmed combat, up to swordplay." That should work well. "As it is, you're going to be sore tomorrow, working muscles you haven't really worked before."

"I'm already feeling a little sore," he said with a grin. "I don't mind it. It means I've done something." He stopped his practice and faced me. "I don't suppose you'd want to show me an advanced move? I'm just curious."

I grinned. "You sure?"

He nodded.

I shrugged. "As you wish. Throw one of those punches at me, full speed," I said. When he raised a brow, I smiled even wider. "You remember how fast I am from last time, right? Don't worry, I'll be fine. Go ahead."

He shrugged, set himself, then jabbed with his right arm. He was fast, but not fast enough.

I easily grabbed his wrist with my left hand, then stepped in, turning and ducking under his arm, twisting it, while remaining in front of him. Then, with a bit of pressure to that locked arm, he fell back. I followed him. I didn't *have* to end up on top of him, straddling him, but I did, holding his arm up as we both huffed out a breath.

"Whoa!" he said, blinking.

My heart pounded. A part of me wanted to lean down and kiss him.

Was that a flash of arousal in his sea-green eyes? If so, he blinked and it was gone.

"You're..." He swallowed hard. "...Amazing. That was amazing. Can you release me now?"

Right...

When I let go, he flexed his arm and hand. I stayed on top of him a moment longer, enjoying the feel of a man between my legs, even if there was far too much cloth between us. I restrained myself from rocking my hips over him, but gods how I wanted to grind down on him, ride him like a fancy stallion.

"I hope someday I can get *you* on *your* back," Leo joked, then seemed to realize what he'd said. His eyes went wide. He seemed about to stumble over an apology when I cut him off.

"I look forward to it." Wow! That had come out all husky and breathy, with a lot more innuendo than I had intended. I cleared my throat and tried again in a more instructor-like voice: "It'll mean you've learned your lessons well." I got off him quickly and rose, helping him up. I hoped he hadn't noticed.

I still didn't know if he wanted me in that way, but more and more I felt a strong attraction to him. It had something to do with how gentlemanly and courteous he was, with his "Miss Tisera" this, and "Miss Tisera" that.

He listened to me, did as I asked. He *respected* me.

And he wasn't intimidated by me.

No man had treated me like that, not since... Kel.

It was because Leo was my student, but still, some

men would have balked and questioned everything. Leo never did. Also... Leo was gorgeous. All that together meant a part of me really wanted to rip his sweaty clothes off and ravish him.

I should ask him, right now, just get it out and see how he felt... but suddenly all my bravery and bravado fled. My throat closed up, and words wouldn't come.

What would I say? I was blunt and crass and I didn't think, "Hey, wanna fuck?" would be right for him. So... I didn't say anything at all. The moment passed and I was his instructor again.

"That's it for today. If you want to clean yourself up, you can pull some water from the well. Daz or Avela can help you if you need it. I desperately need a bath."

I turned and left, hurrying to the juniper grove. I did want to get clean and soak, but I also desperately needed a release. My nethers were aching for a cock, but my fingers would have to do.

Not that long later, slumped low in the bath, I envisioned straddling Leo once again, only this time we were sweaty for a different reason and there were no clothes between us.

Gods! I desperately wanted that man!

I just had to figure out how to ask him...

...And hope he wanted to be with me too.

CHAPTER 10

Leonin

By Halea and her heavenly courtesans!

I watched Tisera walk away, all passionate power, her training clothes stuck to her strong, lithe form. Then she disappeared around the corner of the house on her way to have a bath.

Gods, how I wished I could join her. I wanted to run my hands — slick with soap — over her naked form, while she did the same for me. We'd cleanse each other then merge our passions while floating amidst the waters, and...

...I had to stop that fantasy now, before my cock tore free of my trousers. A moment before, when she'd been on top of me... she must have felt how aroused I was. Perhaps that's why she'd hurried off?

Had I shamed myself?

No... I... I think she'd liked it? The way she'd said *I*

look forward to it, after I'd made that horribly inappropriate comment about *getting her on her back*, had been so very suggestive, like she wanted me on top of her for... other reasons. Alternately... I might have been a bit delirious with pain from my twisted arm and imagined all of that.

But I hadn't imagined my own arousal. I was still hard and ready. I couldn't get the image of her on top of me out of my mind. She'd been all hot intensity, her shirt clinging to her form, showing her high, tight breasts, and narrow waist. She was beautiful and strong and... unlike any woman I'd ever known.

"Amazing," I breathed, then sighed heavily.

I shouldn't have been fantasizing about her. She was my instructor, a teacher. Yet, we were both adults. There should be a reasonable way to enjoy a social relationship outside of our contractual one. I just had no idea how that worked. It was not something which had come up in any of my studies. And Tisera specifically was vastly different from any woman I'd ever known. I had no clue how to even approach her.

Almost all of my interactions with women — before now — had been carefully arranged by my mother. They had been restrained and courtly, two words which did not describe Tisera.

Luckily, I had been married for two years and had learned a lot about women in that time. It had been our duty to have an heir. Yet it had not been easy for Theodora to conceive, which meant... we had tried *a lot*. Still, as much as I'd learned to help her enjoy the act, our coupling had often been a bit perfunctory and mandated, which cast a shadow over it. Something told me sex with Tisera would be anything but perfunctory.

I stood there, staring at where she had been for a long time before shaking myself out of my reverie and making my way back to the yard on the other side of the house. I'd brought a change of clothes, expecting to get sweaty and dirty in the heat of the summer's day. But first, I'd need a bit of a bath myself. When I found the well, I saw another man sitting nearby, on a bench in the shade of several trees.

"Are you Daz?" I asked. "Tisera's brother?" She'd mentioned her brother in passing a few times.

The man nodded. "*Adopted* brother, yes. And you're her new student?"

"Yes, Leo. A pleasure to meet you."

"And you." He gave a breath of a laugh. "It looks like she ran you ragged. Need some water?"

"That would be amazing, yes, thank you."

"The well's right there, you can draw it yourself," the man said with a wink.

I laughed. I was a little too used to people doing things for me. None of that happened here, and it was quite refreshing.

I pulled up a bucket of water and dumped it over my head, dousing myself. After a second one of those, I turned back to the man. "Where might I change?"

"Up in the cottage is probably best. A man like you wouldn't use a barn, would you?"

"I would prefer not to."

"Yeah, the cottage should be fine."

I nodded to him and made my way back up the path

beside the garden toward the small house. Oddly, the man rose and followed me.

"Not that you made a bad choice, but what made you choose Dizzy as your instructor?" he asked.

"Dizzy?" I asked back.

"Oh, right, Tisera, sorry. Most of those who know her call her Tisi. I modified that a bit. She is dizzying when she fights, isn't she?"

"She is indeed. It is a very apt name for her. As for why I chose her..." I hesitated to tell the truth — that no one else would teach me — and instead went for something more tactful yet still true, even if I hadn't known it at the time.

"The male instructors I've known tend to think everyone is the same. They were taught one way and so they teach others the same way. And if you're not built like them... you don't do well. Miss Tisera, however, is very insightful and teaches me in a way which is best for me. She can see my strengths in addition to my *many* weaknesses and helps me build on the former while working on the latter. She's quite brilliant, and very skilled at her trade."

"That is all true," Daz said, just a bit wistfully.

He waited outside the cottage, leaning against the outer wall, while I changed. When I came out, before I left, I turned back to him.

"Thank you for your hospitality." Then my curiosity got the better of me. "You're Dazar Stormhold, the Phorasti who ended the Siege of Vestrea, aren't you?"

I'd known he was a Phorasti when I'd first seen him, since he'd been in full robes. Yet his hood had covered his face so I hadn't seen his darker, soft-brown complexion, which was clearly Dathi. A few Pearlians had learned the ways of the Phorasti, and when Tisera had said he was her brother, I'd assumed "Daz" was one such mystic. It hadn't been until I'd seen his features and heard he was adopted that it had sunk in for me.

And as much as there were a few other Phorasti in Pearlia, Dazar was the only one of any real power. A *true* hero of legend!

Dazar grimaced. "That's not what I want to be known for, but yes."

I shood my head. "I can't believe *you're* Tisera's brother. What a family!"

Dazar gave a wry smile. "*Adopted* brother," he said, emphasizing that word once again. "Dizzy's father took me in after the war... The Dath-Riven War that is."

I nodded. "A kind man, was he?"

Daz cocked his head. "He was a warrior, through and through, but with a heart too large for one made for war."

A fascinating description of a man. I nodded again.

Suddenly Dazar's eyes went wide and he straightened from where he'd been leaning against the house. His entire demeanor changed in an instant from relaxed power to attentive submission. I was curious what could have brought about this change.

"Hey boys. Talking about me?" Tisera said from behind me.

I turned and immediately turned back, averting my gaze. Tisera strode from that odd doorway among the trees wrapped only in a towel! It covered her torso but left far too much of her legs uncovered. And by-the-gods her legs were amazing, rounded and strong.

I was instantly hard once again, trying not to picture what was under that towel.

She walked right past us and into the house without another word, though I did hear a faint chuckle from her.

And with my gaze averted as it was, I got a very good look at Daz's reaction to her. I instantly knew: he loved her, not like a brother loves a sister, but in the way any man can love any woman.

In the next instant, I realized something else... given everything I'd seen: Tisera had no clue how Daz felt.

I straightened once the door had closed. "She is beautiful," I said softly, low.

"She is," he said with wonder, before catching himself. "... my sister, she is my sister and..."

"And you love her, don't you?" I said, keeping my voice hushed.

He blinked. "How...?"

"It's plain as day... to everyone but her, apparently."

Daz sighed and the spirit went out of him. Deflated, he leaned against the wall again.

"She's seen me as a brother for so long she can't see me any other way. But I've *always* been fascinated with her, even when we were kids. I just didn't know what I was feeling until I was older and by then... she'd found other men."

"She's not with anyone now, is she?"

"No, but..."

Ah.

He'd been her brother for so long he didn't know how

to change that relationship. It seemed he and I were in a vaguely similar boat. We were both fascinated with the same woman, and both hoped she'd see us as something more than our current roles: brother and student.

It was a good thing I was an honest and upstanding man. Otherwise, I would have competed with this man for Tisera's affections, but he'd known her for far longer. He'd been with her all her life. I couldn't compete with that. So, I would concede...

For now...

"I know this advice may be unsolicited, but you need to tell her how you feel. Tell her before it's too late. That is all I can say. I lost my wife far too soon. And Tisera is in a dangerous line of work. If she were to die without you having told her, I think you'd be quite devastated, wouldn't you?" I laid a hand on his shoulder, man to man, reassuring. "Don't let her slip away."

I turned and left, heartsick, but having done the honorable thing.

I just hoped Daz would do what he needed to do. Because my chivalry had its limits, and if he didn't tell her how he felt soon... then *I'd* tell her how *I* felt.

CHAPTER 11

Dazar

I watched Leo leave, a bit stunned at how easily he'd seen right through me.

He was... very odd indeed.

His colors lingered where he'd stood. I don't know what he'd been feeling, but it had been *intense* and had left a bit of an after-image once he'd departed. His deep purple hue wafted around me, the intensity intoxicating. Blues and violets were already fading, but they had remained a moment as well.

I blinked, bringing myself back to reality. Though, even as I regained myself, his words rang through me.

... you love her, don't you?

It's plain as day... to everyone but her, apparently.

She's not with anyone now, is she?

...you need to tell her how you feel.

...before it's too late.

...Tisera is in a dangerous line of work. If she were to die without you having told her...

Don't let her slip away.

I'd never really thought about it. Yes, Dizzy was a warrior, but she'd always returned from her missions. She was that good. But then I recalled something our father had once said to me, about his time as a mercenary:

"Skill and experience will keep you alive on the battle-field... most of the time. But I've seen men more skilled than I felled by a lucky shot from an untrained clod when they weren't looking. Skill will get you most of the way, but the rest is up to Tawandi."

I recalled the conversation clearly because I'd been impressed that he'd known the name of a Dathi god: Tawandi of wind and storm... as well as chance and fate.

Suddenly I was terrified. Dizzy had two new jobs, protecting some noblewoman and training this noble-man, and either of those might result in some unlucky incident and...

Gods, no!

I had to tell her.

I couldn't wait. Leo was right.

I rushed inside the cottage and barged into her room. She never locked her door, she didn't need to... but that meant I arrived to find her barely-dressed.

I froze, my eyes going wide and jaw dropping as I stared at her... mostly naked.

She had one leg lifted, drawing buckskin leggings up over it, but wore... nothing else. Her posture, leaning forward, emphasized her breasts, which were usually not so prominent, but now they hung, full, below her. I couldn't help but admire the shapely curve of her buttocks and the long, strong line of her legs.

"Ah... hey Daz. What's up?" She didn't even *try* to cover up. Neither did she continue dressing. She must have been a bit stunned as well. Yet, it spoke to how comfortable she was around me, that she didn't think she needed to cover up.

But that didn't help. My cock went hard in an instant. I couldn't stop staring at her. She stayed bent over, with a confused, bemused smile.

Tell her! Now! My mind screamed at me. *Tell her you love her, then go in there and...*

The image was *very* vivid: I imagined saying the words with confidence and passion, then I stripped and went to her. She remained as she was, slightly bent over, as I took her from behind and we both screamed out our bliss as a heady, mutual orgasm swept through us.

"Daz?" she said again. This time she started moving. She slid on the buckskin pants, finishing with her one leg and stepping in with the other to pull them up. Yet, she remained topless. Her lean, athletic physique called to me: taut stomach, narrow waist, the high soft swells of her breasts. Strong muscles covered her shoulders and lengthened down her arms. She was... amazing!

Though I didn't work my body nearly as often, nor as aggressively as she did, I was naturally tall and well built. Controlling the colors meant having control of one's body as well and my time at The White Tower had included some physical training. We were a perfect match. I wanted — no, *needed* — to tell her I love her.

But the sight of her naked before me had befuddled me thoroughly. Lust raged through me, sending all my blood flowing out of my brain and into my cock and I just couldn't form words. I stammered out something completely incoherent, even more embarrassed by that. How had this gone so wrong?

I couldn't do it, not here, not now, not with her half-dressed. So I backed out and closed the door.

And when that door clicked shut, my cowardice crushed me like a tidal wave. I'd had my chance to tell her, but I'd failed. And a part of me didn't know if I could ever face her again!

So, I ran. I infused red and orange into my muscles and bones to sprint faster than any man could. I bolted, out of the cottage and away: down the lane and out into the city. I didn't stop until I hit the river, at the end of a dock with several fishing boats tied to it.

I could go no farther, so I screamed out my frustration.

I hadn't been able to do it. Even with all the urgency and impetus that Leo had instilled in me, I'd frozen then ran.

I told myself it had been because she'd been half naked, but the truth was, I didn't know. Perhaps, even if she'd been dressed, I'd have run away, a true coward, unable to express my feelings to the woman I loved.

I screamed again and slammed my fist into a tall post at the end of the pier. But I still had my body infused with strength and vitality, so I shattered the eight-inch-thick post, sending splinters and wood fragments flying in all directions.

Several fishermen around me shouted and called out in alarm, though, luckily none were hurt.

I shook my head, letting the colors seep out of me, my shoulders slumping. This was who I was: a coward with strength he didn't deserve.

How could I ever face Dizzy again?

She was perfect: strong and sure and beautiful, even if she didn't see it. I'd thought, after my last breakdown — after she'd asked me to warm her bath — that I'd come to terms with just being her "brother." I'd be there for her in every way she needed me to be, cooking and doing all things domestic. I liked doing those things for her, but now...

I just...

How could I go back after I'd run off like that?

Sighing heavily, I turned and slunk back through the city. I'd find some inn and stay the night. Tomorrow I'd sneak back to the cottage while Dizzy was out and gather my things. I couldn't be around her anymore.

She wouldn't want me.

She was fearless.

And I was a craven fool. I didn't deserve her.

For all my power... I was a wretch of a man.

I wept then, hot bitter tears as I made my way through the city in shame.

CHAPTER 12

Tisera

I was concerned about Daz.

I hadn't seen him since he'd run off yesterday. He'd seemed shocked and ashamed after walking in on me changing. I didn't know why. We'd grown up together and seen pretty much everything there was to see when bathing as youths. Sure, he was bigger now and I assumed all parts of him had grown, even if I hadn't seen them, but... what did that matter? We were family. We were close.

When I'd been in Drako's Dragoons, I'd been the only woman, so I'd done as the men had done. I'd bathed and camped with them. They'd seen all of me. Some of them had been awkward about it, but it wasn't as if there was a women's area for anything, so what choice did I have? Eventually most of the men in my company had become like family. I'd been "just another guy" to them.

For my part, I'd learned not to care much for my modesty. I was a warrior. Warriors didn't have modesty.

I'd thought it the same with Daz, but it seemed perhaps, he didn't see it that way. Was he really that sensitive?

Perhaps?

"What are you thinking about? You've been quiet all morning." Veora's words brought me out of my reverie and I smiled at her. We were returning from a morning visit with the prince. It was just before noon and the city bustled with activity.

"Nothing," I lied. "Just... family stuff."

"You haven't said much about your family," she said. "What are they like?"

I smiled, realizing we were just about to cross Outer Ring Road, the wide boulevard on which I lived.

"Would you like to meet them?" I asked. "We're not far from my house. I could make you lunch. Though my lunches are nothing spectacular. If Daz is there, he'll whip us up something amazing. He's my brother. He's who I was just thinking about." But... would he be there? He hadn't returned after running off yesterday. Hence why I was worried for him.

"Oh! That would be wonderful. Yes, I'd love to see where you live," Veora replied with a wide smile.

"This way then," I said, turning onto the road. She followed and soon enough we were at my long lane.

"This is where you live? It's lovely!" Veora gushed. "I love the trees and the lawns. I wouldn't have expected this inside the city."

Avela and Shorine waved, tending to sheep on my front lawn.

I waved back.

"It's not much. And the cottage is nothing compared to your manor house, but it's home. My grandfather bought this land off a destitute nobleman," I said as we made our way down the lane toward the cabin. "He liked having nature around him, but didn't need much of a house, so... this is it."

"Still, this is truly lovely! An oasis within the city. You're very lucky to live here."

"Daz?" I called as we entered the cottage.

Silence.

I went to his room, but hesitated before entering, remembering yesterday. The difference between us was, I didn't care if he was naked or not, so I went in.

What I found within baffled me. His room was made up and serene and... several of his things were missing. When I checked his wardrobe, most of his clothes were gone, as was his travelling bag.

Had he been called away on another urgent mission as a Phorasti?

That must be it.

I sighed and hoped he was well.

"Sorry," I said to Veora as I returned to her. "Daz isn't here. He must have been called off on Phorasti business. That means it'll be a simple lunch."

"Phorasti? Truly? Is he powerful?" She was a bit agog at this.

"I don't really know. He says he's a Master, whatever that means."

"Oh! That *is* impressive."

"Is it?" I didn't really know. He'd never really talked about his abilities.

All I knew was that when my father had taken me from Aunt Emri — eighteen years ago — he'd had with him a small Dathi boy. Father had told me I had a brother now. We'd been raised together for four years before Daz's abilities had grown in strength and he'd gone off to The White Tower to study. When he'd returned, about nine years ago, he'd been a man, and a Master Phorasti, whatever that meant.

He'd been called away on missions now and then, and when the latest war had broken out, he'd been called to The White Tower once again, while I'd gone off to fight.

Our father had died while we'd both been away. I'd returned to an empty house. That memory still stung, especially since that had been right after Kel had abandoned me.

Daz had returned home roughly two years ago. He'd been tense and tight-lipped, refusing to say anything about where he'd been or what he'd done. But then... that wasn't new. He'd never told me anything about his work.

Since then, he'd been a fixture in my life. Even when he'd gone away on Phorasti business we'd sent letters back and forth. And when he was home, he did everything for me. He liked the day-to-day stuff, which I agonized over. I truly appreciated everything he did for me.

If he was some powerful and impressive mystic, he'd

never said a word about it. But then, he'd always been quiet and modest.

"Perhaps he'll be around some other time and I can introduce you two," I said to Veora. "Now... for lunch."

We ate a simple meal, but I still had some of the exotic fruits from our market day, so we finished them off.

Veora sat back in her chair with a sigh. "Tell me, Tisi, is there a man in your life? You seemed to know that man who came with Victor the day we met."

Ah yes, Kel.

I sighed, contented, from the sweet food and pleasant company. Could I tell her about Kel? I hesitated as she hummed softly to herself, a habit of hers. Then I shrugged. Why not...

"Yes, and no. There's no man in my life now, but Kelric, the man you met that day, was a part of my life, long ago. Then..." I shrugged. "I don't know. The war ended and so did our relationship."

"Oh?" she asked, curious.

I nodded. "I... I wouldn't say we were ever in a *deep* relationship, but... I guess I'd hoped we could be."

The memories filtered back to me. So much of that time I didn't want to remember. The Siege of Vestrea had been... horrific.

Kel had been the one shining light in that abysmal Hellscape.

"We were lovers and... very passionate." I blushed a bit admitting this, but Veora made me feel so comfortable that it passed quickly. She didn't judge, just listened.

"The war was... horrible and our moments together were all that kept me sane some days. We were in the same mercenary company so there wasn't much privacy. But we'd sneak away to dark corners and... ah... well, you know. I thought he loved me."

"I sense a 'but'?" she asked.

"Indeed." I sighed. "When the war ended and the siege on Vestrea was lifted—"

"Wait, Vestrea? You were at the siege of Vestrea? I hear that was horrible."

"It was." And that was all I'd say on that.

Yet listening to Veora's soft humming soothed me and I found myself going on.

"We were all happy when the armistice was called and we could go home. But our company had to stay for a little longer to oversee some of the aid coming into the city."

I drew in a long breath. This was the hard part. "One day Kel... he came to me and kissed me passionately with a strange smile on his face and... and said he'd be back, but nothing more about where he was going. Then... he vanished."

I shuddered out a breath then forced a smile, telling myself I wouldn't cry. I'd cried enough over that man and hated every tear.

"I thought he'd return later that day and when he didn't, I asked his father, Drako, the leader of our crew, where Kel had gone. He said he didn't know, only that Kel had asked for special permission to leave and hadn't said when he'd be back."

"I waited for him for days, but he never returned." I shook my head at the heavy memories, swallowing around a lump in my throat.

"I was devastated. Even though the war was over, I was surrounded by so much desolation and death and horror that I'd needed some comfort. But he'd disappeared. He'd *said* he loved me, then... he abandoned me when I'd needed him the most!"

My voice had risen, so I drew several long breaths to calm myself. My expression turned sour. I wasn't proud of what I'd done next.

"I was so lost and uncertain. My sergeant found me crying my brains out. He held me close and whispered some kind words and... I'm ashamed to say... I'd needed to be with *someone* so I... took some comfort from him that night."

I grimaced.

"That turned out to be a mistake. He was not what you'd call a patient lover, nor particularly skilled, but he'd been a warm body next to me in the darkness and that had helped."

I sighed heavily, shaking my head.

"As for Kel, he never returned as far as I know. Some of the crew said he'd come back at one point then left again, but I'd never seen him. That was it. He'd deserted me when I'd needed him most. Then, when our company finally returned to Pearlia, he was here. Apparently, he'd been here all along. I couldn't face him, and he couldn't face me. So, we left it at that."

"That's horrible, Tisi. I'm so sorry." Veora reached across the table to take my hand. Her warmth and compassion helped to restore me to myself as I wiped a single tear from my eye with my free hand. I loathed remembering those hard days.

"It's nothing really. I'm well over him now." I smiled.

We chatted for a bit longer before I escorted Veora back to her house. Walking home again, I realized I felt far better than I had in a long time. I'd never thought telling anyone about Kel and the war would help, but it had.

I smiled and even hummed to myself as I returned home, very much looking forward to my training with Leo later today.

CHAPTER 13

KELRIC

IT WAS GRUELING WORK REMAINING CONSCIOUS WHILE listening to the monotone voice of General Hiset, the royal military advisor. This man had never seen real action, despite being a general. He knew tactics and strategy well enough, but he'd gained his position through politics and not through surviving one rough situation after another, like I had.

But I was on his turf, called to this royal advisory council, with Queen Helena listening intently at one end of the large table. What this man had to say was important and could affect me and my company. So, I tried not to fall asleep as he droned on.

"...which is the fourth incursion this month. They are not coming far into Pearlia, and they daren't threaten any of our farmers. No, they do it just to see if they can, to see if we'll respond."

The small man sighed heavily. "And they have completed yet another fortification along the river. They now have nearly twenty such towers." He shook his head. "My men are worried. They fear another war with Eromore. And I cannot tell them it won't happen. The Eromorn are power-hungry fiends. They will not attack until they are ready, but I fear they shall be ready soon. And when they are, they may need only the slightest provocation, if that, to invade us once again."

I couldn't help myself. "They didn't invade us last time," I said stoically. "We annexed one of their provinces through a political marriage."

Silence hung over the room. No one else here would ever speak to General Hiset in such a tone.

"Yes," the man said, a little perturbed. "And then *they* invaded our newly acquired territory."

"The captain's point is valid." This from the queen, her aged voice still strong, a resonant alto. "We provoked them, and they responded." She looked at me intently then. "But we will not be doing that again any time soon. We'll give them no reason to attack us."

The question we were all considering, though, was: did they need a reason?

The queen sighed heavily. "It's Ossara I'm worried about. The way my son has abandoned his wife is disgraceful."

Prince Victor was in the room, at the table, but the queen wouldn't even look at him.

I grimaced. I was fairly certain the queen didn't know how I'd facilitated her son's continued tryst with his mistress.

I was beginning to regret that choice. Word was, the princess's family back in Ossara were not happy about how the prince had treated her. There were fears he would discard his family in favor of this mistress and have a new heir. I didn't think Victor was the type of man to do that, but then... he'd seemed different these past few months since he'd met Veora, more distant from everyone except his mistress. I didn't know the man well, but as the captain of a mercenary company that was now fully in the employ of the crown, I had spoken with him on several occasions. I'd thought the man to be courteous and gallant, but perhaps I'd never truly known him.

When I looked over at Victor, his face was shadowed with defiance. He spoke stiffly.

"Princess Kira wants for nothing. She is well tended and loves our children, but she'd spurned our bed for far too long. I simply wished for some company now and then."

"Perhaps if you tended to her as you did to your mistress, your wife would join you more often, princeling." The queen's tone was harsh.

That silenced Victor, who remained stoic after that.

I tried not to shake my head. I hoped I'd done the right thing helping him to continue seeing his mistress. Not that I could have denied the prince his request.

The queen turned to General Hiset. "What is our preparedness, General? If Eromore does attack, how would we fare?"

I knew the answer to this, and wondered what the general would say. "Our forces were depleted in the last war. We'd be able to defend any fortifications. They wouldn't take the capital..." He hesitated.

The queen finished. "But they'd take the rest of our nation, yes?"

"Yes, Your Majesty."

"That is unacceptable." A hardness set on the queen's already stern features. The silver hair and the wizened lines on her face seemed chiseled from stone. Her steel-blue eyes reflected a soul which had seen far too much hardship already.

"What of the Phorasti?" she asked. "How many more could we call to arms?"

There was only one Phorasti of any real power in the city... Tisi's adopted brother, Dazar. I'd gotten to know him when I'd been apprenticed to her father. He was a good man, though I hadn't seen him in years. But I'd heard how he'd been instrumental in lifting the siege on Vestrea and ending the war. If one man could do that, then perhaps an army of them could...

"From our latest information, there are nine Phorasti in the city, most are Pearlians who sought training at the White Tower. Unfortunately, it seems non-Dathi do not fare as well in learning those mystic arts. A few of our Phorasti could be useful as healers, but most have little ability. The only true Phorasti in the city is the Dathi man who helped us end the last war. It is my hope he would come to our aid, if needed."

"Only one?" The queen did not seem pleased. "What about the other Dathi at the White tower?"

"Your Majesty, the Phorastic Council has said they

will not participate in any conflict. They said that Phora is the energy of life, and to use it to kill is abhorrent."

The queen's jaw twitched. "I don't particularly like war either," she muttered. "Do they not realize they only have the liberty of their high ideals because we freed them?" she hissed.

Pearlia had fought with the Free Dathi during the Dath-Riven war, against the Purists, a movement of full-blooded Dathi who'd sought to eliminate any half-Dathi and mixed-bloods. It had been a brutal and grueling conflict ranging over many lands — since the Dathi, once a nomadic people — had settled amongst many nations.

I knew of the war only through tales from my father. It had ended almost twenty years ago, when I'd been just a boy.

After the war, some of the Free Dathi had built The White Tower in Pearlian lands: a place to train those with the gift to see and manipulate the energies they called Phora. The crown had given them those lands, helped them get set up, and supported them. Now they had turned their backs on us?

This was news to me.

The queen didn't seem happy about it either. Yet, she settled herself quickly, jaw still tight.

"I suppose we did free them so they could pursue their own ways. I can't fault them for hating war. I hate war." She slumped into the high-backed chair and sighed, running an aged hand over her features as she recovered herself. Yet, I could see she didn't like any options before her.

She spoke slowly, as if the words themselves were bitter.

"If we began a conscription campaign, how many able men could we gather and how quickly could they be trained?" It was clear she didn't like the option.

She then gave a nasty grin. "And the *first* to be conscripted would be the nobles. They should be leading the way in all things in this nation, war included."

She practically snarled her next words. "They've all grown soft and indolent. *They* should be the ones protecting this nation, but they've been safe from war for so many generations this current band of fops couldn't fight off a cornered kitten." She sighed heavily, then glared at the general, clearly expecting an answer to her previous question.

"Ah..." He had no clue, but I did.

"Your Majesty? If I may?"

"Yes, Captain, please."

I rose. "I've had experience taking on new men. Now... these were men who *wanted* to fight. Even so, it takes at least six months to train a man well enough to survive the heat of battle, but in truth, that won't be enough. If we're conscripting men, they might be able to defend themselves after six months, but they'll probably run at the first sign of trouble. Especially these *indolent fops* you're hoping to recruit. What we're lacking are veterans."

The queen's features shifted slowly: one brow raised and the corner of her mouth twitched. "*Your* troop are veterans of the last war, are they not?"

I sighed, knowing where this was going. "Yes, Your Majesty."

"Have you considered my offer to join the royal guard?"

I had... and I was still undecided.

Right now, I was working for the crown, true enough, but it was a contract. I was still a mercenary captain in charge of my own men. I could disperse them as I wished. I was the one in control. If I joined Her Majesty's forces, I'd no longer be in control. I'd be working for generals like Hiset. True, I'd be paid a lot more and I'd still be a captain to all my men, but...

Perhaps, I could counteroffer? But I didn't want to do it here.

"I have been considering your offer Your Majesty. I wish to speak to you about it in closed quarters, if that serves you?"

"Yes, we shall speak now." She turned to General Hiset. "Is there anything else?"

"No, Your Majesty," the man said stiffly.

"Then leave, all of you." The words were soft but forceful. She waved her hand and the others immediately began to disperse. I, however, stayed.

I remained standing as the others filed out and the door was closed.

"You wish to counter my offer?" the queen said, shrewd as ever.

"Yes."

"Then go on, say it."

"You said yourself you're in need of veteran men. If I were to join the royal guard, that would not be enough to change the direction we're heading. I would need to *command* the royal guard, and I'd need to disperse my men to positions I see fit for them to lead and direct those around them. And I would suggest you do something similar with the other mercenary companies currently under your service, but... *I'd* be in charge of *all* of them. I'd be your Field Marshal, commanding your armies."

She gave me a hard look.

"If it were your father making this request, I'd accept in an instant. And I mean that as no insult to you." Her words were quick but precise.

"But *you* are a boy. You may be a veteran of the last war, but to put you in charge... I'd have a mutiny on my hands. My commanders would leave me. They're all from respected noble houses and I need the support of those houses, even if their sons are barely able to swing a sword." She sighed, looking down. "What you ask is... difficult." Then she looked up at me, those eyes capturing me. "But I will consider it."

That was surprising and frankly more than I'd expected. She must be truly desperate.

"Thank you, Your Majesty."

I bowed and left, feeling more than a little shaky. I'd asked for the command of Pearlia's armies, and what scared me most was...

...I might actually get it.

CHAPTER 14

TISERA

IT HAD ONLY BEEN A DAY SINCE LEO'S LAST SESSION, BUT he'd improved. He must have been practicing all night. I didn't know what else nobles had to do, probably nothing, which might explain his free time to train. Yet he was sore today, that much I could tell.

"Your left arm is weaker today, but your form is excellent," I said watching him.

"Thank you, Master Tisera."

When I'd told him it sounded odd for him to be calling me 'Miss' all the time, he'd taken to calling me 'Master' instead. The curious part was, he didn't say it with any irony or sarcasm. He meant it. Though he did smile in a special way when he said my name.

"This is my one goal, I will do whatever it takes to excel in this, Master Tisera." That much I believed entirely. He had to be sore from yesterday, but he hadn't complained once.

"We're done with review," I said. I hadn't intended to move on so quickly. I'd been going to reinforce the basics, what he'd learned yesterday, but he had clearly studied well and deserved a reward. "We'll move on to some blocks and redirects."

"Yes, Master Tisera," he said, relaxing into a ready stance.

"We'll move through these slowly, as you attack me, so I can show you what I'm doing, then I'll attack you, slowly, so you can try it." I set myself. "Attack but keep it slow."

Leo stepped in and, shifting his full body as I'd shown him, threw a punch at my face. I talked through my block as I did it.

"This is a simple block, but you can do it four ways, depending on what you wish to do next and which arm you use. The simplest version is to push your opponent's arm away while you step to the side."

With my right hand I did a slow slap block, pushing his wrist to my left as I stepped right.

"Also, I can grab your arm, if I wish." I wrapped my open hand around his wrist. "For more advanced moves." I gave a quick tug to pull him off balance. He stumbled forward a step. I caught him, my hands on his shoulder and chest, his body close. Those sea-green eyes caught mine and his gaze held.

We remained like that for what seemed like an eternity, but it was only the span of a few heartbeats.

"Tisera," he whispered, and the soft breath of his voice sent a shivering thrill through me.

"Yes," I replied, just as breathy.

He blinked and the moment was gone. "Ah... sorry... Master Tisera. Thank you. What's next?"

I regained myself quickly, not sure what we'd just shared. My heart slowly calmed as I continued the lesson.

"You can use either hand and push in either direction. Throw another slow punch and I'll show you."

We went through that sequence of blocks, then he tried them and did well in the slow-motion instruction. "Now we'll speed it up a little." We did the sequence again as I attacked faster and faster, until we seemed to be reaching his limit. "Now block with just the right arm." Again, he did well. "Now the left." That was slower and weaker, but he had the technique down.

I stopped. "You're doing very well," I said with a grin.

He beamed. "Thank you, Master Tisera." He huffed out a heavy breath. "I know you'd do really well teaching women." Before I could object, he continued. "Would you mind if I brought a few to our next session?"

I grinned. "If you can find interested women, then by all means." I didn't think he'd find any. I was fairly certain few women wanted to be tough and strong. Being tough and strong certainly hadn't been easy for me.

Leo nodded. "I will."

I went over a few other block and evasion techniques. By the end of our time, Leo was running through simple combinations of attacks and blocks.

I watched with appreciation and pride. So, this is what it felt like to teach someone and have them completely absorb your instruction. I was impressed with Leo. I could tell he really wanted this.

"That's it for today," I said. "We should take a break for a few days. I can tell you're sore and you're going to be even more fatigued tomorrow. Come back in three days. Until then let your body rest and heal and keep practicing what you've learned. You're coming along well, Leo."

He bowed solemnly to me. "Thank you, Master Tisera." He was all formal courtesy and a part of me loved it.

Leo treated me with respect, a gentleman through and through. It was... refreshing. Most men either recoiled from me because I wasn't womanly enough, or — if they didn't know me — treated me like they treated most women, which wasn't well. Then there was Kel, who'd abandoned me. And Daz, who was always so awkward, which was adorable but a bit tiring after a while. Leo was different. For the first time, someone saw me — all of me — and accepted me.

I hesitated then, wanting so very badly to invite Leo back to have a bath with me, knowing I wanted more than just a bath.

But... I couldn't. He was such a perfect gentleman and student, and I didn't want to ruin that. I simply nodded to him.

"Tisera," he said softly. He seemed hesitant, as if he had something to say, but was unsure of himself.

I waited, curious and a bit nervous. What would he say?

"I..." He sighed. "I... really appreciate everything

you've done for me. I know I can find more students for you. You're an amazing instructor. Thank you, Master Tisera."

I smiled. It hadn't been what I'd hoped, but it was kind and wonderful nonetheless.

"You're welcome. Would you like to use my bath, to clean up... before I do?"

He smiled. "No, thank you for the offer, but I'll be well. You go, enjoy yourself."

I would.

We parted and I headed for the bath. Daz still hadn't returned, so I'd have to settle for a tepid one, but it was a warm enough day that I didn't mind.

While I bathed, I fantasized about a school of combat for women, where women came from all over to train with me. They were all perfect students, like Leo, and learned quickly. I was truly helping people and making a good living out of it, which didn't involve the possibility of dying... nor killing.

And that was truly a wonderful thought.

CHAPTER 15

TISERA

THIS TIME I WASN'T INSIDE THE CARRIAGE, BUT RIDING IN the footman's position, standing on the back, hanging on to a heavy bar with one hand as the vehicle moved from the main road to the rougher track heading north.

I kept a warry eye out. No one should know the Heir Apparent was out of the capital, but that didn't stop me from being cautious. Prince Victor had managed to sneak out of the palace for an afternoon in the countryside with his love, and I was their *only* guard.

His logic had been sound: a massive contingent of men might have been safer but would have drawn much more attention. As it was, any passerby would think him only some fancy noble with his wife, not the crown prince.

Still, I didn't like this one bit. I had a bad feeling about this excursion. From within the carriage came Veora's giggles and sighs. It seemed the two of them couldn't wait to be together.

The carriage pulled off the road where a grassy field nestled between the road and a burbling brook. On the other side of the road were farmer's fields, flat lands with no one about for miles except herders and plowmen. Rising from the far side of the brook was a pleasant woodlot. Overall, it seemed a fairly innocuous and safe location, but still, I was on edge.

I jumped off the carriage, sword out and ready as I walked the perimeter of the site. I was in full battle armor, a chain mail shirt with full sleeves and a four-segmented skirt which fell to the knee, for easy move-ment. Over that I wore a breastplate and back-plate, pauldrons, and bracers, with a helm covering my head. On my legs were padded leggings under sturdy steel greaves on my calves and winged poleyns over my knees. It was heavy, but I'd trained for years in this and even heavier armor to make sure I could go for hours without tiring.

The carriage driver laid out blankets and pillows, along with the extravagant lunch, while the two lovebirds remained in the carriage for now. Only once everything was prepared and I'd given the all-clear did they come out.

Veora's dress was already undone and loose on her. She was flushed and giddy as she pulled up the shoulder of the dress, which had slipped down exposing some skin. She and the prince sat on the blanket, ignoring the food, returning their attentions to each other. The carriage driver made his way to the other side of the carriage so the two would have some privacy and I... patrolled.

The afternoon wore on as the prince and Veora inter-mixed play with food. I remained vigilant, trying to ignore the grunts and moans and sighs and cries.

Something — a flash of movement within the shadows of that woodlot across the stream — caught my attention.

I peered more intently and saw it again.

It might have been some wild deer, but I'd still check it out.

The brook rose to my knee at its deepest, but I managed to avoid sloshing through it by hopping from stone to stone. The opposite bank was higher, so I grabbed a low branch from a tree to pull myself up. Once on the other side and within the confines of the quiet woodlot I put a tree to my back and listened.

Birds chirped and wind tousled the leaves and branches above me. It seemed like a perfect summer's day. Quiet...

Then came the soft snap of a twig, barely audible, but caught by my keen hearing.

My sword was already out, but I drew my long parrying dagger in my left hand as I listened more intently.

Someone or something was out there... more than one. Four... no... five creatures made their way slowly and quietly toward the stream. Deer didn't move like that. Not even wolves moved in such a formation.

No, these predators were of the human variety. And that... most likely... meant bandits: an opportunistic group hoping to rob a nobleman. I couldn't fathom a political attack all the way out here, with all the secrecy we'd maintained.

I grinned behind my helm. Today was about to get a lot more interesting.

I'd always been quiet and careful, even in heavy armor. I darted from one tree to another, closing distance with whoever was out there.

I caught another flash of movement...

Close.

The time for stealth had passed. I strode forward with all the subtlety of a charging bull, toward a small clearing where three men held crossbows, all pointed at me.

I didn't want to alert the lovers, so I kept my voice low when I said. "Hello, boys."

The thrill of the fight filled me. I stood poised and ready, my eyes and ears piqued for any movement.

"We don't want to kill you. We just want whatever them nobles got on 'em. Surrender and you'll survive."

"That seems a fair deal, so I'll make it back to you: Surrender and you'll survive."

One of the men laughed. But the two others didn't. That told me who the newbie was in the group. One of these three still thought this was going to be an easy fight, a game. The other two were the ones to watch.

Pure energy, like a raging fire, filled me as our stand-off grew more and more tense. If they hadn't fired already, they were waiting for something. Most likely that would be one of their companions out in the woods attacking me from behind.

The rustle and crunch of some groundcover behind me was the only warning.

I spun, sword out, and took the man who'd been sneaking up on me clean across the throat. I darted back into the woods as he fell. A geyser of blood, spurting from his neck, splashed over my shoulder as I ducked behind a tree.

Crossbow bolts thudded into the tree behind me as one passed by into the woods beyond.

One down, four to go.

I spotted the fourth moving in the shadows. He was trying to avoid the fight and get to the prince and Veora. That wasn't going to happen.

The other three were still reloading their crossbows, not a quick weapon, so I took that time to run after the fourth.

He heard me coming and turned, setting himself for a fight. He had a sword — which looked rough, not well cared for — and a wooden shield. He wore heavy padding and a helm, but not much else in the way of armor.

"Stop this and I'll let you live," I hissed as I drew close and paused for an instant to gage his reaction.

"You're a woman?" he said, then laughed.

That was not the right answer.

I lunged in low and sliced the inside of his thigh before quickly returning to my ready stance. I cocked my head, hearing the other three crunching through the woods behind me. I had to end this quickly.

"Fuck!" the man swore and as a reaction slashed wildly at me.

That had been what I'd hoped for. I caught his heavy downward slash, stepping in. He didn't know how to properly defend himself and he'd shifted his shield to the side for his attack. So, he was wide open for my dagger, which I sunk to the hilt into his arm-pit under his sword arm. I drew my dagger out quickly and a gush of blood followed. The man screamed, but I'd punctured his lung and there was little force behind the death-cry. Just in case he still had something left in him, I hacked off his sword arm as he slowly collapsed.

A crossbow bolt hit me, a glancing blow off my helm, which was incredibly lucky, but still made my head ring. I dove to one side, but not before another bolt hit me low in the back. Since I'd been diving it too was mostly a glancing blow, but it tore a small chunk out of my armor and my side before it left. That's what I got for staying in one place too long.

Pain sparked through me as I hit the ground and rolled away. Yet, with a battle-haze upon me, I hardly felt it. What little I did feel only served to spur me on, turning the fire inside into a raging inferno. I rolled quickly to my feet and charged in at the remaining three before they could reload.

Two were experienced and tossed their crossbows aside to draw swords. The last one — the one who'd laughed — tried to reload.

I roughly hacked the crossbow from his hands, then flicked my sword up across his neck. He seemed extremely surprised as he died.

The other two both seemed to know how to hold themselves in a fight, spreading out to either side of me.

They both wore patchwork armor — they'd seen tough times, clearly — but their swords were well tended and sharp. It wouldn't surprise me if these last two were veterans of the last war. Perhaps their mercenary company had disbanded and they'd drunk away their earnings? I didn't really care. They'd made the poor decision to attack the people I protected. They'd pay for that.

Both tested me, lunges from either side, I deftly danced and blocked their tentative strikes. They could clearly see I was no one to be trifled with.

"It's her," the one said. "The woman from the Dragoons!"

That's right.

"Yeah, so? I don't care if she is as good as any man, she can't take the *two* of us together."

We'd see about that. I'd already killed three of their comrades.

"And she's wounded," the other said, considering.

That was true, and I was losing blood. I couldn't afford to let this fight draw out... so, I charged one of them, turning my back on the other for an instant. Hopefully, I'd be fast enough to have one clean engagement with this one before they were both on me again.

My slash was wild, meant to keep him back as I got to the other side of him, but he was quick and managed to not only block my sword, but knock it down and away. I brought it back quickly, but not quickly enough. His sword came down on my sword arm and crunched against my chain mail. My arm gave even as I struck him as well, a blow to his left side. We both staggered away from the encounter with a grunt. My sword arm was half-numb and growing weaker. I didn't see any blood welling up from under the chain links of the armor, but that didn't mean he hadn't done significant damage.

I retreated a bit farther into the woods and ducked behind a tree.

"Get her!" This a cry from the wounded one. "I got her sword arm!"

He had.

So, I put my dagger away and moved my sword to my left hand. It was a very good thing my father had trained me relentlessly in sword-work with both hands.

The man came crashing through the forest. I spun out from behind the tree and caught his sword on mine, flicking it out and away to one side. But what I hadn't seen was the dagger he'd gotten out and held in his left hand.

I reached up with my weak arm and caught his arm as it descended, but I had little strength and only succeeded in slowing the blow, redirecting it a bit so the main force hit my pauldron, not my head. The narrow blade skittered over my shoulder and down the chain on my already wounded right arm. It caught on a link and bit into armor and flesh. A line of fire seared along my arm. It wouldn't be deep, but it would weaken me all the quicker.

I brought my sword up, hacking into his right side, but he flung himself away at the same time with a cry.

Then the other one, wounded and staggering, came in again. I raised my sword to block his, but the blades met at an odd angle and my blade was knocked from my grip. Luckily, he was over extended, and his sword came down too hard sinking into the earth.

My right arm was next to useless, but I stepped in and punched him with it. It would only daze him, doing no real damage, but I used that time to pull out my dagger with my good arm, slashing it across his throat. He gurgled and fell back, lifeless.

The other man roared as he came at me, sword out. The blade hit the flare at the bottom of my breastplate and dented it thoroughly, but then slid off to one side.

Wounded as he was, he was quick and brought his sword up to block my slash with the dagger.

Then he tackled me, knocking us both to the ground. He was on top of me, but I kicked and rolled, turning the tables to straddle him. I'd lost my dagger, but my left fist would do well as a weapon. I hammered it down into his face three times before he tried to lift his sword. His attack was weak, his arm at a bad angle. I knocked the blade away with my bracer, then punched him again, harder. He groaned and went still, but he wasn't dead, still breathing hard.

"Do you yield?" I asked, my voice raw and hissing.

"I do," he said, though his nose was broken and he sounded like he was choking on his own blood.

I got up, slowly, unsteadily. "I see no need to kill you, but you'll die soon if that wound in your side isn't tended.

I found my sword and dagger, plucking them up. My right arm was bleeding and useless, my side throbbed with agony, and my gut — where my armor was dented — felt like someone had punched me. But overall — with five on one — I'd fared well.

As I staggered away, the man breathed, "By the gods, she's a demoness!"

I grinned.

Damned right.

The coachman was cleaning up the picnic as I sloshed through the stream, not able to skip so lightly across the rocks this time.

He looked up at me as I strode toward him. "By the gods!" he hissed. "You—"

"Are well enough. Just clean up quick and hurry back to the city. I could use a healer in due time, but most of this blood isn't mine."

He blinked at me and nodded, redoubling his cleaning. We were soon on our way.

The lovers were laughing to themselves inside the carriage. They would never know what had happened to me nor what had almost happened to them.

And that was how it should be.

CHAPTER 16

DAZAR

MY QUIET DESPONDENCE WAS INTERRUPTED BY AN insistent knock on the door. Only one person knew I'd fled to this modest inn.

"Avela?" I asked.

"Yes, Master Dazar, please hurry!"

I sighed, rose, and went to the door, opening it. Avela looked a mess, bedraggled and fatigued. Had she run here?

When I'd gathered my things and left the cottage, I hadn't gone far. I hadn't known what to do, where to go, at least not yet. So, I'd gotten a room at a pleasant inn called the Blue Goose, about a five-minute walk from the cottage. I'd told Avela where I'd be in case of emergencies. It seemed... there was an emergency.

"Mistress Tisera is hurt, she needs healing. You need

to come quickly!" Avela said, breathless and clearly distraught.

I left without a second thought. When I looked back at Avela, she waved me away.

"I'll follow in time, go!"

I ran.

I gathered my aura and pushed strength and vitality — red and orange — into my legs, heart, and lungs as I sprinted back to the cottage. Horror consumed me when I saw blood spots all the way down the lane and into the house. I followed them in shock, hoping — praying — Tisera was still alive.

I burst into her room, like I had yesterday, only this time she was not naked and proud, she groaned, sitting on her bed, trying — with little success — to remove her armor. Her right arm hung limp and she bled from a gash in her side. Her aura was all over the place — fluctuating and erratic — as her life energies floundered and surged in a wild dance of life and death.

"Let me help," I said and rushed to her.

"Daz?" She seemed confused, her voice raw and weak. "Where...?"

"Don't worry about it. Just lay back. I'll get this armor off."

She relaxed a little, falling back on her bed. Her eyelids fluttered shut as she let herself finally rest.

I removed the armor carefully. The breastplate had a significant dent in the front which looked like it wouldn't be comfortable at all. And the metal of the back plate had been pushed into a deep gash on her side. It looked nasty. I couldn't imagine what sort of weapon might have caused this, nor did I want to know. I cautiously removed the breastplate, managed to roll her onto her front, and got the backplate off without doing any more damage.

I summoned green for a quick assessment of her injuries: that nasty gash to her side, several wounds to her right arm, a bump on the head, and bruising where her armor had been dented in. Fever and delirium had set in as well. That would be easy to sooth away, once I'd dealt with the physical issues.

I focused my aura on that deep and messy cut low on the right side of her abdomen. First the hardest part: I summoned white, purity, to cleanse the wound before I healed it. White wasn't so much a single color as it was *all* colors, which meant it took a lot to channel. Concentrating, I carefully cleaned the wound. Then, I brought forth green for health and recovery, and red for strength, and some orange to encourage the flesh to mend. Sweat dampened my brow by the time that was done.

With her worst injury mended, I could take a moment to recover and plan which wound I'd tend to next. My sense of Dizzy's Phora had given me a pretty clear picture of the damage, but I removed the rest of her armor and clothes for a closer physical inspection.

Dizzy woke from her feverish mumblings as I sat her up to remove her shirt.

"Taking advantage of me, are you?" She didn't know who she was talking to, her eyes lidded, gaze unfocused.

When she did manage to focus on me, she whispered, "Daz?" then swooned and went limp again.

I laid her down. I didn't need to remove her leggings, her legs were uninjured, just fatigued. Yet, her upper half was naked to me so I'd be able to see the results of my healing.

As much as a part of me wished to see her unclothed, this was *not* what I'd had in mind. At least I handled the sight better this time than the last.

I grimaced at that remembrance as I moved my hands over her slowly, just above her skin, doing one final assessment of her condition.

Her right arm was my primary concern now. The bone was fractured, nerves pinched and crushed. A long cut marred her biceps muscle, and under that the skin was a livid purple. Her forearm and hand were nearly white, blood wasn't flowing to them.

I set to healing it. This took deeper work, feeling the colors of the tissue itself and mending it slowly and carefully. I set the bone and knit together the muscles, nerves, and skin.

Once the arm was healed, I tended to the small bump on the back of her head and the bruising on her stomach.

After that, I laid a blanket of green and aqua Phora over Dizzy to help reduce the fever and let her rest.

I finished and sighed. I'd been kneeling next to the bed, so I slumped over, laying my head on the mattress and rested.

My exhaustion swelled. I'd worn myself out, not only from the healing, but from the extremity of emotion I'd felt when I'd thought her to be dying.

"How is she doing?" Avela asked tentatively from the doorway.

"She'd have lasted for some time still. She's tough enough to withstand more than this, but... thank you for getting me. She's resting now. And I... I'm going to rest too."

Avela nodded with a smile.

I turned away and set my head down again on the soft mattress.

"Daz?"

I started awake.

It was dark outside. A lantern had been lit, flickering low, and a pitcher of water and a tray with food sat on the table next to Dizzy's bed.

It took me a moment to realize who'd spoken my name. I looked up at Dizzy. She lay on her side on the bed. She hadn't bothered covering up. Smiling down at me, she whispered, "Thank you. For... patching me up. I... don't remember much."

I met her gaze in the dim light. "I love you," I said, and instantly realized I'd said *those* words. I froze.

I'd said it now.

She smiled and laughed. "I love you too." She reached over and ruffled my hair. I took her meaning instantly. She loved me like a brother. Slightly more seriously she said. "You're always there for me."

I couldn't go back on my words now. Leo had said I needed to tell her soon, because she was in a dangerous line of work and I'd not heeded him. But I'd just seen how dangerous her work could be. I couldn't hold back any longer.

"No, Dizzy. I love you. Not like a sister, but... but like the fields love the rain, like trees love the sun, like..." These metaphors were nice, but she was a direct woman.

I should be direct. "Like a husband loves his bride. Like a lover loves his beloved."

Her eyes grew wide.

I pushed on. I couldn't stop now. "I know we were raised like brother and sister, but we are not blood. I'm Dathi and you're Aestrian. I know our paths have taken us apart more than they've brought us together, but... but that's just it, Dizzy... Tisi... Tisera." I sighed.

"I can't lose you like I almost did today. I... I need you to know how I feel... even if that makes things awkward between us. I'd rather be awkward than live a lie."

"Daz," she whispered. I could tell by her colors she was stunned and confused, my revelation had thrown her. Her aura danced around her, wild and discordant.

She looked away, still not covering herself.

After a heavy sigh, she gave a bit of a laugh. "That... explains a lot. Like the look on your face when you came in on me dressing. Gods, you looked like you'd swallowed a squirrel." She sobered. "Wow... ah... this is a lot."

It was. I rose.

"If you need some time, I can leave and come back." I got as far as the door before she called to me.

"Daz?"

I turned back, trying not to see... all of her. "Yes?"

"Is this why you... packed up your things and left?"

I nodded. "It was just... too hard to be around you. I tried to tell you and couldn't. And I couldn't live with my cowardice around someone so brave and strong."

She nodded slowly. "I... I hope you'll come back," she said, but her tone sounded like she was questioning herself. Maybe that was a question for me. If so:

"I will. I always will."

She nodded.

"Take as much time as you need," I said softly. "You're still recovering from your healing and... now you have this to think on. I'll go get my things from where I'm staying and return."

She nodded.

I left, walking taller than I had in some time. I'd finally done it. I'd told her I loved her. I still didn't know how things would work out, but that didn't matter so much as the need to have this out in the open.

Now everything was in her hands.

I hoped she felt the same way... or at least would come to, given time.

Yet, when I returned with my things later that night, she was gone, her bed empty.

CHAPTER 17

TISERA

I COULDN'T REST, TIRED AS I WAS. DAZ'S REVELATION HAD left me stunned, with a mind too whirling and boggled to sleep. I rose and threw a shirt on, not bothering to change out of my leggings. I didn't plan to go far.

Daz's healing had left me feeling energized. Fatigue would set in again soon, but after the rest I'd had that afternoon, I felt good enough for a bit of a walk.

I left the cabin and my feet led me to the small, one-room hut next to the barn, where Shorine and Avela lived. Despite the late hour, I could see light through the windows and knocked lightly on the door.

Avela answered. As she did, a grumbling voice from within mumbled, "Talk outside." Shorine must have been trying to rest.

Avela grabbed a light shawl and the small candle-lantern she'd had lit and slipped out.

"Mistress Tisera, I'm glad to see you well." She looked a bit haggard and worn herself.

Some distant part of my memory — feverish and hazy as it had been — recalled seeing her as I'd stumbled down the lane and into the house.

"Did you... get Daz?" I asked softly, making that connection now. "Did you know where he was?"

She grimaced, clearly abashed. "I did, yes." Which answered both questions. "He was so distraught when he left. He said he'd be at the Blue Goose for a few days. That he needed some time and space to think about things." She looked at me directly then. "And by *things*, he meant you."

Oh.

Avela and I sat on one of the benches under the trees beside the well. "Did you... know... how he felt?" I asked.

"Yes." She sighed heavily.

"I..." I couldn't quite make sense of this. "Aren't you and he...? You spent so much time together in the garden and you're a beautiful woman and... I just assumed he saw you that way and..."

She laughed a little. "I... *was* interested in him, yes, but he never felt the same for me. He's always loved you. My charms were lost on him."

"I find that very hard to believe." Avela was the picture of womanly beauty: a perfect hour-glass figure, curved and full, with that gorgeous blond hair and golden eyes, like a sunrise.

"You may not think yourself attractive, but he's completely taken with you," she whispered, then drew a deep breath.

"He told me once how he sees you. He spoke of colors, of your deep reds and vibrant oranges. His mystical training gives him another way of seeing the world and through that, you are... truly a beautiful woman to him."

"Huh," I said, a bit distracted. Daz didn't see the world quite like other people. He'd told me a bit about the colors and auras and stuff, but...

Slowly it sank in. He did... anything and everything for me. He cooked and cleaned, he tended the garden and occasionally helped with other chores around the grounds. I'd thought he was doing all that because that's what interested him — and maybe it was — but I could see now, he was doing them for me as well.

And... it wasn't like he wasn't a handsome man. That bronzed skin and thick, dark hair. His soft, caramel-brown eyes, and a body, which was broad and tall. He was fit and strong, even if it wasn't battle-trained strength. And the way he smiled at me: always so open and free and... loving. I'd thought it a fraternal love, but now...

"Oh..." I whispered.

"You can see it now, can't you?"

"Yes." I shook my head. "I've been so blind. I've been an idiot!"

"You've been distracted and not seeing him as he sees you, that is all. Now that you do... what will you do about it?"

"I don't know," I said honestly. I still didn't truly believe he could love me like that. I didn't believe *anyone* could love me like that.

Kel had been a lover, but those had been trying times,

when the heat of our coupling had banished the darkness for a moment or two. Some of the other men in my troop had lain with each other to do the same thing. I'd just thought... we'd been like that... just another troopmate. He'd never really *loved* me.

I wasn't built for love.

I was built for battle. That's what I'd trained my entire life for. Other girls are taught ways to attract a man, to live with him and work with him and be with him. I was taught how to kill a man or protect him if he was on my side.

Avela laid a hand on my knee. I looked up at her, those golden eyes and her bounteous beauty. Why would any man wish to be with me instead of her?

"You still don't think yourself worthy of love?" she asked softly. She had always been perceptive. "Not beautiful?"

"No," I said plainly. "I don't."

"You need to take a long look at yourself in a looking glass someday," Avela said. "There is a lot more to you than your work. You're tall and proud, strong and sure. Some men like a woman who knows what she wants and is sure enough to go and get it."

I was nearly certain that *wasn't* the case, but I let her go on.

"Your features may not be as soft as some women, but you are far from unattractive."

She moved a hand up to brush back some of my wild hair. "Some men like a bit of a wild look to their women."

She gave a breathy laugh. "And though your cheeks and chin and nose are a bit... sharp, they are not unappealing." She traced a finger down the side of my face. "Your lips are full, with a natural tinge of red, which many men find beautiful." She flicked her finger off my chin. "And you are not portly, nor old. Your body is fit and you have enough of a bust for men to see you're a woman... when you're not in your armor, that is."

I looked at Avela, curious. The way she spoke made me think *she* was fond of me.

She must have seen something in my look for she smiled broadly, with a hint of her own blush. "You know what I did before Shorine found me, yes?"

I did. Her life had not been easy at all. She'd been sold to a brothel by her parents as a child. She'd done other duties until she'd been old enough to bed a man, then she'd been put to work in the usual way. She had not been specific about her time at the brothel, but I could see it had left its marks upon her soul.

Then she'd caught the waning sickness, which had lingered within her and she'd not been able to see customers. Despite her beauty, she'd been a burden on the business and the mistress had cast her out into the streets. That's when Shorine had found her and brought her in, nursing her back to health. Avela was one of the lucky few who had come through the waning sickness regaining full health.

She went on. "Well, not all of those who visited me... were men."

Oh... That I had *not* known.

She smiled softly. "So... I have learned to see beauty in many faces."

I shouldn't have asked, but I was too curious now,

"What... is it like? Were there any you were with who were good lovers? I... I've never..."

I'd only ever been with one man, Kel. And our couplings had been to push away our fears and sorrows, physical and immediate, hard and needful. I'd never been with a man in the way others were: soft and sensuous and loving.

She looked away. She didn't like to talk about those days and I shouldn't have asked.

I quickly said, "I'm sorry, you don't—"

"There were a few," she whispered. "Men who had truly fallen for my charms, who brought me gifts and fawned over me." She smiled faintly. "And... sometimes, one of the other girls would come to me. We'd... comfort each other. It was through her that I'd come to know... *all* the ways to be loved."

She gazed off into the darkness, drawing long deep breaths before going on. "I don't know if I loved any of them, but I could feel their love for me and that was... nice. The touch of a lover, of someone who seeks only to bring you pleasure can be *very* rewarding."

She hesitated. "I... I could... teach you, if you wish?"

"No," I said softly. "That is not your job here and I'd never ask it of you. I truly appreciate the offer, but..." I shrugged. "If a man ever does love me that way, than I'm assuming I'll know."

Avela laughed lightly. "Oh yes, you will." She looked at me then. "Daz would love to show you."

I smiled.

Curious, I brought to mind the image of Daz with his shirt off, round muscles on a lean frame. He had *many* handsome features, but... to think of Daz being with me as Kel had been... even if it was soft and loving... was still a little too weird.

But then... Maybe Kel was my problem.

Maybe I couldn't imagine being with any other man because part of me was still stuck on the pain that Kel had put me through. I had fantasized a little about Leo, but a part of me had been terrified to approach him. And Daz... I didn't know what I wanted from him, but... What he felt for me was far different than what Kel and I had shared.

Kel... hadn't loved me. We'd had lust and heat and passion and need. Picturing myself with anyone else in the same way — which was all I'd ever known of sex — just seemed odd and awkward.

"Thank you, Avela," I said and patted her knee. "I know what I need now."

"If you ever need to talk about... anything, I'm here, mistress. You and Shorine have been an amazing blessing upon my life. I am happy to help any way I can." She rose, nodded to me, and — taking her lantern — returned to her house.

I sat, lingering in the darkness.

I knew what I needed to do. I needed to face Kel and get rid of the stain he'd been — and still was — upon my life.

I rose and strode purposefully away, down the lane and across town. It was only much later that I realized three things: first, it was the middle of the night and Kel was probably asleep. Second, I was still in my padded-armor-leggings and must look a mess. Third, my fatigue would soon return.

I shrugged that off. It didn't matter what time it was, nor what I looked like, I was going to have it out with Kel once and for all. And my determination gave me the energy to overcome my exhaustion as I marched off into the night.

CHAPTER 18

Tᴉsᴇʀᴀ

I ᴋɴᴇᴡ ᴛʜᴇ ᴛᴡᴏ ᴍᴇɴ sᴛᴀɴᴅɪɴɢ ɢᴜᴀʀᴅ ᴏᴜᴛsɪᴅᴇ ᴛʜᴇ Dragoons' compound in the third ring of the city. "Harik, Beson." I nodded to them. "I need to speak to Kel... now."

I must have looked like quite the sight, and certainly my tone didn't allow for any questioning. Perhaps the late hour also lent a bit of immediacy to my demand, I wouldn't be coming now if it wasn't important.

Harik nodded and slipped inside without a word.

Beson nodded to me. "Tisera. Long time." Beson had never been one for long speeches.

I responded in kind. "It has."

And that was the extent of our conversation.

Harik returned soon enough. "He'll see you," Harik said. As if he'd had a choice. "You know where his room is?"

"Did he take Drako's old room or stay in his own?"

"He's in his own room. Drako's is empty."

I nodded and strode into the compound. Harik closed the door behind me.

I made my way through dark and quiet corridors to Kel's room. I didn't know if he'd been up or if Harik had woken him, but faint light outlined the door. I didn't knock, just went in.

Kel's room may have been large compared to some of the other quarters in the barracks, but they were far from extravagant: a standard bed and large wardrobe, three stacked chests on one side of the room, the other side held a large desk. Kel sat behind the desk, a lantern flickering before him. He motioned to one of the three chairs in front of the desk.

"Tisera," he said softly.

Interesting. He must have also sensed that I wouldn't have come now if it wasn't important. He'd used my full name, not Sera. He hadn't tried to goad me.

I looked at the chair, but I couldn't sit. Instead, I went and grabbed the back of it, leaning forward a little. "I've come for the truth, Kel."

He raised a brow. "Which truth would that be?" he asked, his tone cool. I could see his perceptions shifting. He'd thought this was business but was becoming aware it wasn't.

"I need to know, Kel, where did you go when you left Vestrea?" My throat constricted, my jaw tightened. "You... you left me and you never came back. You... What the fuck did you do? What was so important? Why did you leave me!" I couldn't stop myself from shouting.

He blinked at the vehemence of my outburst, but his

surprise only lasted a moment. Then his face turned hard.

"Is that what you think?" he said. His jaw twitched. "You thought..." He laughed, a harsh thing. "You thought I left you?"

"You did!"

He slammed his fist on the desk, then rose in a rush, leaning forward, looming and outraged.

I matched him stare for stare. I didn't know why *he* was so upset.

"You're the one who shacked up with Sergeant Tomas the instant I was gone!"

I blinked.

"Tomas?" That threw me. Yes, I'd had a single — not particularly rewarding — night with Tomas, but only after... "You'd been gone *five days*!"

"And that's all it took for you to forget me!"

I blinked again.

This wasn't going how I'd thought it would. I needed to take control.

Charging out from behind the chair, I circled around behind the desk, next to Kel. He was taller than me by a head, but that didn't stop me from getting up in his face.

I spoke quickly, giving him no room to break in.

"No, Kel, *you* left. You said you had something you needed to do, and you'd be back, but you didn't say how long. You didn't say you'd be gone for one day or two, let alone months! I waited for you, first for hours, then one day, then another."

A righteous wrath filled me as I railed at him. "You say five days like it was nothing, but it was an *eternity*!

Vestrea was an open wound. It was horrible. I *needed* you and you weren't there!"

Feeling the need to do more than just shout, I punched him — not *too* hard — in the shoulder. It didn't make me feel any better.

Tears leaked from my eyes as I tore more of those vicious memories from my soul and spoke them aloud.

"I'd been shredded by... by... you *know* what we went through! And I'd thought maybe our moments in the dark had meant something. But then you left and took my heart with you and never came back."

Tears streamed over my cheeks, despite my desire to contain them.

"Yes, I had *one* less-than-satisfactory encounter with Tomas, but that was because I needed something from *someone* Kel. And. You. Weren't. There!" I poked his chest hard with each word.

"Those five days felt like five *lifetimes* for me. The war may have been over, but I needed you more than ever and you'd run off, never to return! What the fuck, Kel? What the gods-damned bloody *fuck* was so important? Where did you go?"

His shoulders fell, the fight going out of him. He looked at me, mouth agape but with nothing to say.

Ha!

Yeah!

That was how this was supposed to go, none of this *"You're the one who shacked up with Tomas"* shit.

"I'm sorry, Tisi," he said softly, slowly, swallowing hard. "I... I didn't know. I thought everything was good once the war was over. I... *did* want to be with you." He turned away, ashamed.

Gods-damned right! He should be!

"You want to know where I went?" he asked, voice low.

"Yes!" I bit out, harsh and furious.

He whispered, "I went to ask your father for your hand in marriage before he died."

I staggered back, as if I'd been gut-punched, followed by an upper-cut to my jaw. I reached out for the wall, but it was too far away and I fell, collapsing.

No...

Five days... Two days hard ride from Vestrea to Pearlia, one day here, then two days back.

No...

Kel turned back slowly. He continued in that soft voice.

"And I got back just in time to find you... in that tavern outside the city... with Tomas. I returned with your father's blessing and found you..."

Oh... gods... no!

My mind whirled.

But confusion sparked my anger again. I surged to my feet.

"Why?" I shouted at him, voice hoarse and cracking. "Why didn't you *say* something? Why didn't you tell me what you were doing, how long you'd be gone? I could have waited if I'd known... But instead. As far as I knew, you left and never came back! You abandoned me!"

His jaw tightened and he let out a harsh laugh, though it sounded a bit self-deprecating.

"We both failed each other, it seems."

He fell back into his chair, heavy and tired. "All I had to do was tell you where I was going, and all you had to do was wait just a little longer. By Aestric and Assa! By all the gods we were so close and we... gods, we fucked it up royally."

The fight left me as quickly as it had returned. I swallowed hard.

"So... you saw my father... before he died?" He'd been gone by the time I'd gotten back to Pearlia.

Kel nodded.

"He was weak, so far gone, it was... it wasn't easy to see him like that." Oddly, a flicker of a smile caught his lips. "But even through all that. When I asked him for your hand, he smiled and sat up and took my hand as if he was ten years younger and not on his deathbed."

Kel's gaze was distant, remembering. "He nodded and said it had always been his hope that you and I would unite. He gave his blessing and smiled and..." He sighed heavily. "I don't know for certain, but... he seemed so at peace after that. I think it allowed him to let go and find the peace in Assa's Arms he'd been seeking for years."

I turned away to hide the new tears in my eyes.

One of the horrible parts of the waning sickness was how slowly it ate away at a person. My father had only begun suffering from it when the war had started six years ago, and it had taken him two full years to die...

...While I'd been away, fighting the war.

I'd not been there for him. It still ate at me after all this time. But Kel had seen my father and... and brought him some peace, which it seemed had allowed him to let go and pass on... but that also meant...

"You... if you had waited." I choked back sobs at the pain searing my heart. "If you had stayed with me and we'd returned together... perhaps I'd have been able to see my father one last time."

I shouldn't blame Kel for my father's death. But I'd come here to yell at him, to have things out once and for all, to get rid of all of the pent-up pain. And this was just another affliction I needed to express.

He sighed heavily. "You don't know how many times I've wondered the same thing. I... I thought I was doing the right thing, but I messed everything up." He sounded defeated.

Good.

I spun on Kel again, the pain of not being with my father when he passed a new fuel for my anger. My shouts now were nearly incoherent through tears and snot and a throat swollen with emotion.

"That's right! You did! It's all your fault Kel! It's... How could you!" I wanted to keep going but the fatigue from Daz's healing, which I'd been powering through, finally caught up to me. I stumbled, falling forward.

Kel was up in an instant and caught me. And when he did, those strong arms gathered me close to him and held me tight.

I hated him and loved him for it at the same time.

I pounded my fists against his chest and wept onto his shoulder, mumble-shouting meaningless words. The words didn't matter, he just needed to know how I felt.

"I know," he whispered. "I'm so sorry, Tisi."

I stopped pounding on his chest and let myself melt into him, supported by him, held and warm and...

No...

No! I didn't want to be comforted, not by him, not now.

I pushed away violently and almost fell back. This time I did manage to catch myself on the wall.

Gods, I was weak as a kitten. I shook my head slowly.

"No," was all I managed to say, though I didn't really know what that meant. I only knew I had done what I'd come to do, but this hadn't gone how I'd imagined at all.

Knowing his side of the story only made things worse.

I rushed out as fast as my staggering legs would carry me, slamming the door behind me. I stumble-ran, wiping my tears on a sleeve, so very thankful no one else was about in these dark halls.

Kel didn't follow.

Part of me was very glad.

Part of me broke a little more.

Gods, I was a mess. I'd come here to sort myself out and now I was a hundred times worse.

I'd hoped I would be able to face Daz after I'd talked to Kel. I'd hoped I could come to terms with Daz's admission of love, but that, added to everything else, only made my emotional load all the heavier. I couldn't deal with any of this!

I burst out from the compound, past Harik and Beson, and fled into the city.

I didn't return home, I couldn't, not yet.

I found a dark alley and alternated between heaving sobs and punching walls. Neither made me feel any better.

CHAPTER 19

Kelric

I stared at the door for a while after Tisera had left.

I was...

Gods! I was as much a mess as she was.

I sat heavily in my chair behind the desk and stared at my hands, at anything, as long as I didn't have to think.

Yet I couldn't help but think.

What had I done?

Had it been me or her?

True, I hadn't told her where I was going, but at the time... the war had been over and I'd thought she'd been well enough. She'd been my rock during the siege, nothing could break her. I hadn't told her... because I'd wanted to surprise her... but gods, that was just idiotic! Why hadn't I told her? Why hadn't I just said, "I love you, Tisi, marry me, let's go see your father before he dies."

Why?

I didn't have a good answer. I'd made a mistake, a massive mistake. I'd left her and I'd — in some ways — taken her father from her.

And though those five days had passed quickly for me — excited and riding hard, a plan in my head and love in my heart — I could see how five days might be an eternity of waiting if she didn't know what she was waiting for.

Shit...

... But still... how could she have fucked Tomas?

I shuddered.

It had been petty of me, but as soon as my father had handed control of the Dragoons over to me, I'd given the man his walking papers. I couldn't stand to be around him, let alone work with him.

But she'd only gone to Tomas because she'd needed someone. She'd wanted me, but I hadn't been there. And apparently, he hadn't been the best lover. I took some small solace in that.

But still...

How had I messed things up so badly?

By not communicating, that was how.

It was that simple.

I'd been excited and — for some unknown reason — wanted to surprise her, but I hadn't asked her what *she'd* needed. I'd wanted to get the blessing to marry her as soon as possible, but what did it matter if her father had blessed us? She was the one that mattered. Why had I not asked *her*?

Gods, I was an idiot.

And now... I'd asked the queen to make me a general. How could I be a general if I couldn't even handle one simple situation with the woman I loved, if I couldn't say what needed to be said?

Groaning, I rested my head on my crossed arms on my desk, sighing heavily.

"Captain?"

The voice roused me from a dreamless sleep. I lifted my head — instantly regretting the position I'd accidentally fallen asleep in — and groaned.

"What?" I said a bit too harshly.

"It's well past breakfast," Midros, my aide-de-camp said, standing over me. "Usually, you're up by now. Is everything well?"

"No, everything is not well!" I barked at the poor man. He didn't deserve this. I sighed. "Sorry, Midros. I didn't sleep well."

The man's look said he saw that clearly enough. Thankfully, he said nothing.

"Please bring me some breakfast, whatever you can find. I'll eat here."

The man nodded. He hadn't been dismissed so he waited.

"And..." My mind was heavy and hazy. "What do I have on my schedule today?"

"You have an inspection of the new recruits this morning, a little more than one bell from now. This afternoon is free, I believe you'd wanted to review the provisions and accounting for last month."

Yeah, that wasn't going to happen. I could manage an inspection, but my mind was too befuddled to do heavy work with numbers. "I'll be taking a ride this afternoon instead," I said. "Please make sure that Broadsword is saddled and ready for me after lunch."

"Yes, captain. Is that all?"

"Yes."

Midros left and I rose, groaning again. I just... needed more time to process what had happened last night. I went to dress, then reconsidered, catching a whiff of my own heady scent. I'd have Midros pull a bath for me after breakfast. So... I paced, waiting for my meal, and tried to make sense of things.

For four years, I'd thought Tisera had betrayed me by sleeping with Tomas, but now... Had she?

Or had I betrayed her first by running off without a word?

I didn't really know. As much as I'd made a mistake, I still felt all the pain of seeing her with another man. Even if he'd been horrible in bed, she'd certainly seemed to have been enjoying it. Or perhaps that was just my memory of the event four years later. Perhaps I'd just been so hurt I'd imagined she'd been enjoying herself? I didn't know and no answers lay down that road, so I stopped.

None of this was easy or clear.

I started over again.

I'd made a mistake.

And it had brought about grave consequences. We were both hurt and we'd both been hurting all this time. She'd been brave enough to face me first, to come to me and ask what had happened.

Now we knew.

Last night had been a royal mess, but now everything was out in the open. So... what did that mean?

Was there still a chance for us?

Because everything I'd felt for her had returned when I'd held her close last night. Even if she had been crying and beating on me.

I massaged my bruised chest and shoulder. I would gladly suffer her assault, if it meant I could hold her again.

Gods, I loved that woman.

But I wasn't sure I'd ever told her. Not even in those moments we'd stolen from the darkness during the siege. They had been immediate and hard and needful and afterward, before we'd returned to the barracks, we'd lain together in silence, there had never been any words. But now... I knew. She'd loved me and I had loved her, and we'd both been too closed off to say anything.

And I... I loved her still.

But the question that haunted me as I ate, then bathed, then... went through the motions of the day was: did she still love me?

CHAPTER 20

Tisera

I COULD BE DEATHLY QUIET WHEN I WANTED TO BE. AND since I wasn't ready to speak to Daz, I snuck into the cottage in the hazy light before dawn and grabbed some clothes for the day. Then I had a cold bath — which did wonders to help revive me after a rough night — and left again.

I had to escort Veora to the palace that morning, but I still had time before I needed to get her, so I had breakfast at a rough tavern in the third ring of the city, secretly hoping some drunk would pick a fight with me. Though my bandaged hands and bloody knuckles — from punching walls last night — probably couldn't have taken it.

But still...

And when I picked up Veora, even before she said a word, I launched into a rant about men.

"I don't understand men!" I began, and her brows rose. "They're just so... frustrating and confusing! Some say they love you when you're not expecting it, and some betray you, but not really, because they're trying to marry you, but they don't say anything, so you don't know what's happening and you mess everything up by fucking your sergeant. But it's not my fault he didn't say anything! And... I just, don't understand anything!"

Veora's voice was calm, soothing when she said: "It sounds like what you really don't understand is how you feel."

"I know how I feel!" I said heatedly. But then I deflated a little. "I feel... confused."

"That's not really..." She sighed. "What are you confused about? I don't claim to know everything about men, but I like to think I know a thing or two."

I knew one place to start: "Why do they say things at the wrong time... or... don't say things?" I was still confused, trying to figure out Daz and Kel at the same time.

"Ah... well, *that* I might be able to address."

I was curious and looked over at her.

She seemed to think, lips pursed, perhaps finding the right words before speaking.

"Men can be brave in the face of danger, but when it comes to women, they don't know how to fight that battle. They're feeling things most men don't know how to put into words. It's a lack on their fathers' parts, not teaching them how to be true men and express their feelings. And when faced with a woman, they retreat and run for cover. They stumble over words. They say the wrong thing, or sometimes they say the right thing, but at the wrong time. And even more often, they say nothing at all when they should be saying the most important thing."

That sounded exactly right.

"Men," I muttered.

"Is there a particular man?" Veora asked. "Perhaps this Leo you have mentioned from time to time? Did he say something stupid, or nothing at all?"

Leo? "No... actually. Leo is a complete gentleman." I gave a breath of a laugh. "Actually, when it comes to Leo, I've been the one who's tongue-tied and awkward. I'd like to have a little fun with him, but... I don't know how to say it. He's a gentleman, and... I don't know if he'd be up for a roll in the hay. I don't think he thinks of women or sex that way. But... I know I can't marry him. He's a noble. So... I'd be up for a bit of fun, but... how do I tell him that?"

"Ah..." Veora said. "So... then, who was the man saying the wrong thing?"

"Men," I said with a grimace. "Two of them."

"Two? Two *other* men... other than Leo?"

I laughed. "Yes." She made it sound like I had a whole court of men.

I sobered quickly. I really should talk to Leo. Lack of communication had led to years of pain between Kel and me. So, being honest with Leo seemed prudent.

And Daz had been very clear about his emotions, but I had yet to respond. Here again, if I didn't tell him how I felt, it might lead to pain, for one or both of us. The trouble was, I didn't know how I felt about Daz yet. I needed time, and I assumed he'd give it to me. I just shouldn't take too long.

As for Kel... We'd talked *a lot* last night. Perhaps too much, but nothing had really been resolved. Did he think... there was still a chance for us?

Was there?

I didn't know.

That meant I might possibly have three men who wished to be with me... and who I might wish to be with. That was... complicated.

Fuck me.

"Perhaps if you just tell me everything, I can help?" Veora asked.

So, as we walked, I laid everything out for her: Leo's charm and how that made me feel. Daz's admission of love and how that had thrown me. Then, Kel... everything we'd learned and the truth of what had happened, and that I had no clue what to do now.

"Oh... my," Veora said softly when I'd finished. "That is definitely complicated." Veora looked at me before cocking her head to one side and smiling. "You don't see it do you?"

"See what?"

"That you have at least two men, perhaps three, who are interested in you, who respect you and may love you. I know women who would kill to be in your position, having several handsome men vying for their attentions."

"They're not... vying." *Are they?*

I wasn't the sort of woman who'd have three men after me... and yet, I did.

Fuck me. How had that happened?

"And instead of being surprised and elated and over-joyed that you have a choice of men, you're... upset?" Veora asked.

"Yes!" That much I knew for sure. Although...when she said it that way.

No, I *was* upset! I'd resigned myself to being... unlovable. Given how most men had treated me, I'd always suspected I was different and troublesome at the least. Then Kel had abandoned me and I'd known it. I'd been so sure of it. I'd been certain I was fated to be alone. I'd come to terms with living a simple life, *on my own*.

Only I wasn't alone. Daz had almost always been there for me. I liked that... but now that I knew *why* he'd been doing it... so that hopefully someday I might feel as he did... What was I to make of that?

Did I love Daz?

Yes. I did... in a special way, not like a lover. I loved his caring, his attention, his smile, his laugh, and the comfort of his presence. But having him in my bed?

Whereas Kel... I couldn't *stop* thinking of him and me, half-dressed in some dark corner of Vestrea, grunting and gripping, all physical passion. But I couldn't see him cooking my meals and doing chores around the house.

And Leo... He was the oddest of them all. I wanted him to sweep me off my feet and show me all his passion, but if he did that, he'd stop being... Leo, the upstanding gentleman.

Also, Leo was a noble and there was no way we could have anything other than a fling.

And the thought of him making my meals and cleaning the house almost made me laugh.

So yes, I was frustrated and upset, because my entire life had been turned upside down and none of it made any sense!

I said as much to Veora.

"Oh, I see, that is a challenge, yes."

"With you and the prince, your choice is easy," I said softly. "Either you're with him or you're not. I want to be with each of these three men in different ways. I want to have Daz take care of me, and be soft and intimate with Leo, and fuck the brains out of Kel."

"My situation with Prince Victor is not so easy. I am, to a degree, at his whim. If I deny him..."

I could see how that would be hard. "I'm sorry, I didn't mean to say..." I wasn't sure what I'd meant.

"It is of no consequence, Tisi. I am happy with the prince and if he tires of me, I shall be happy with that, but that is not my choice. You at least have a choice. Perhaps you could... explore *all* avenues open to you?"

"I could?" That didn't seem right. "Don't I have to choose?"

Veora shrugged. "Not if you're open with all of them." She smiled broadly. "Tell them you wish to court them, but that you are not being exclusive. Make it clear others will be courting you. It may give one or more of them greater incentive to be *all* of who you want them to be. And at the same time, you can explore elements of what it's like being with them. Have Kel cook for you. See what sex with Daz is like. As long as you do it with no expectations afterwards, then they can't be too upset if you choose another."

"Oh..." That did sound... curious and appealing. A

shiver ran down my spine. What would it be like to have three men pursuing me... actively? "Oh!"

"Oh indeed." Veora laughed.

"What would I say to them, exactly?"

Veora counselled me on the right words. She was very good with making things seem reasonable.

"Tell them you wish to explore a relationship with them, but that they will not be the only ones. If they balk at this, tell them it is their choice. If they back out now, it will make your choice easier in the end. And if each man knows there are others wooing you, I suspect they will try even harder to win you, and they can't be too upset if another man does more than they do. Be honest, be open, lay it out. Tell them what you wish to try with them and that you will have the final say. Make it clear that if they wish to be with you, this is the only way."

I nodded. That made a lot of sense. I hoped I could remember that.

But... "I don't even know if Kel wants to be with me. We left things a bit... confused and uncertain last night. I did... run out on him."

"And if he loves you then he'll seek you out, or patiently wait for you to return to him."

Yeah, that made sense.

Suddenly I wanted to go talk to Kel right away. Unfortunately, Veora and I were still ten minutes out from the palace and I'd have to wait for her there. I'd go to him this afternoon... No, I had training with Leo this afternoon. And I'd probably see Daz first. I'd talk to Daz, then Leo, then go to see Kel. Yes, that would work.

Gods, suddenly I was more nervous than I'd been for any battle.

Who was I to do this, courting *three* men at once? I was a warrior-woman, not a flirting courtier. Yet my heart raced like it did in the heat of combat. I was going to have three men court me and... I could choose who I wanted.

The only problem was: what if — after all the courting was done — I wanted all three of them?

CHAPTER 21

Leonin

"I've given you significant time, Leonin," my mother said with her usual stern-love voice. The queen was in one of her not-to-be-trifled-with moods. "Have you chosen which priesthood you will join?"

This had been her "offer" for me roughly a year ago: more like an ultimatum. I had a year of leeway, but only to research each priesthood and determine which god I would serve.

I had hoped for more time before she called on me to choose. I wanted to tell her of the work I'd been doing with Tisera and how amazing I felt because of it. But I wasn't ready yet. I still had so much to learn.

I'd been practicing the few moves I knew and trying them in different combinations. They came easily enough, now that I'd practiced the Hells out of them, but I was far from a seasoned warrior.

I needed more time before I presented my counteroffer to my mother.

I didn't know why the combat training I'd been put through as a young man hadn't clicked. Perhaps Tisera was right and they'd been trying to teach me the wrong weapons in the wrong way. I didn't really know, and at this point, I didn't care. Yet Tisera had opened me up to a whole new perspective. I'd always thought myself weak and not the fighting type — and compared to my brothers I wasn't — but now...

Still, I couldn't tell my mother, not yet. I wasn't far enough along. I had to stall, buy more time.

"Mother, I have, alas, only come so far in my religious studies. I have spent much time with the clerics of Aestric and Assa, and learned much from their vast libraries, but there is too much to learn in just one year. I have yet to participate in the rites and rituals of Helea and Olerin, I missed out this past spring, but the mid-summer revels are coming up. I could—"

"Must you?" the queen said, a horrified look on her face.

I'd known that would get a reaction. She didn't want to picture her son naked and lost in a sea of bodies at one of the Halean orgies. In truth, that held little appeal for me, but having always been the studious son. I could easily make the case that if I were to join a temple, I'd need to try *all* of them first, and that included the less savory ones, like Halea, goddess of love, sex, and fertility.

Olerin wasn't quite so bad, a god of nature. Yet his spring rites were — if not overtly sexual — very much full of the suggestion of all the things a god might do to make the land fertile for the coming year. There was even a joint spring rite between the Helean and Olerin Priesthoods which was far more overt. The Mid-summer revels were purely a Halean rite and encouraged all unmarried men and women to try out something or *someone* new... usually many someones, often at the same time.

"If I am to experience the fullness of each priesthood, I should at least try one rite from each. As you know, I participated in the new years' rites of Assa this past year. It would be unfair of me not to try some of the others."

The queen grimaced in distaste but hid it quickly. "If you must." After a sigh, she added, "I would have thought you'd take to the temple of Wisteri."

It was what she'd suggested initially. As a bookish man, the goddess of knowledge did seem a natural fit. And in truth, I loved their libraries, the largest in the lands. But, since I didn't really want to be in the priesthood to begin with, I had tempered my own lust for knowledge and forced myself to try different things.

"I am very curious about the temple of Brovos," I said with a grin, testing the waters a little. "I believe I could become a warrior priest someday, perhaps even a general."

It wasn't unheard of for high-ranking members of the priesthood of Brovos to become generals, since Brovos was the god of war.

"Oh, Leonin, truly? You're still harboring that fantasy?" Her look of complete dismissal stabbed to the core of my being.

I tried to hide how much it hurt. I could be a great general, but she had no faith in me. Even if I couldn't fight, I knew history and strategy and tactics as well as any of our generals.

The queen sighed heavily and shook her head. "Leonin... Leo... my dear son. Don't you see? If you become a general that will only hurt our relationship with Eromore, which already hangs by a thread. They already question your decision to marry Lady Theodora of Vestrea. They only have our word that she wished for the marriage and died by illness, not by other means. Can't you see how it looks if her husband, the man who tore one of their provinces away, went on to become a general? It will seem like we always intended war with them, and you know that's not the case. I need you to be penitent and meek. Join a quiet priesthood and study, you love to study, don't you?"

I sighed. I could see her point, but still, it wasn't what I wanted. "I do, Mother, I do."

"Then do that? Please Leonin, I'm begging you."

"I'll consider it, Mother. I am sorry I am taking so long to choose."

"I'll give you until the end of the summer, no longer." I could see her struggle with her next words. "Try... whatever you must. Take the summer to... get out any of your urges and fantasies. But by the end of the summer, make a choice, please."

"I will, Mother."

I'd just sealed my fate. I had roughly two months to either choose a priesthood or... develop the combat skills others learned over years of training so I could prove my skill as a general.

I left my mother's private chambers and made my way toward my own.

I was stunned when I looked down a long hallway and saw Tisi standing guard outside my brother's rooms. She seemed distracted and didn't look my way.

Which was good.

I slipped away quickly. I didn't want her to see me here. I wasn't quite ready to tell her I was *the* Leo, Prince Leonin. I'd almost told her several times, but I couldn't bring myself to say it. If she knew I was a prince, she might not be as aggressive and forthright in my training, which I needed.

And...

My heart thundered in my chest. Tisera was an amazing woman. I had more than a few fantasies about her. As long as she didn't know who I was, we might be able to dally, but as soon as she knew I was a royal, if I asked her... it would see more like a command, and I didn't want that.

So, I couldn't tell her who I was, not yet. I needed more time with her. I wanted her to know the *real* me before I told her my real name. Maybe that would help.

Though... I'd also promised that adopted brother of hers I'd stay away, let him tell her how he felt. He'd known her far longer than I had, he should have a chance with her.

I sighed.

However, if *he* didn't say anything... then *I* would.

But first, I'd need to do more for her.

I'd promised I'd bring women who might be interested in training. I'd put out feelers and had a few responses. I needed to follow up with them.

I'd go to the library of Brovos and study a little, then sneak out, and go to some of these young noblewomen and see who'd be interested in learning from Tisera. I was certain I could get at least a half-dozen to try a session.

Tisera would be thrilled. Perhaps more than thrilled? Perhaps.

And if that confused Dathi "brother" of hers hadn't said anything by then... Perhaps I'd tell her how I felt.

CHAPTER 22

Tisera

I was distracted by the — very appealing — idea of somehow being with all three of Daz, Kel, and Leo. So, when I caught movement from the corner of my eye, it took me a bit too long to look up. By the time I did, whoever it was had just disappeared around a corner.

I resolved to keep a more wary eye out after that.

But my thoughts were still all jumbled and tumbling, caught up with these three men.

Did Kel still love me?

Did he want more than a physical relationship?

Did I?

Sex with him was amazing, but a life with him, what would that be like? He was a man of action, a man called to duty. Even if I got my act together and started this school Leo was suggesting, Kel would still be going off to war and that would be terrible for me, left behind to worry.

Then... there was Daz, sweet and sensitive Daz. A man of power I couldn't even fathom, yet who loved to cook and clean and make my home a happy, cheery place. We were already so close, how much did I want to be... closer?

The more I thought about it, the more I could see the *possibility* of it. I could see him as a man — a very handsome one — instead of a brother. And I had some — very naughty — fantasies of what he could do with all that mystical power of his.

Leo was... an enigma, but one I very much wanted to take time to solve. He was kind and respectful and charming. As much as I may want him in my bath or bed, naked and gentle and sensuous... I could also imagine us just kissing... or talking. A part of me didn't want to bed him right away. I wanted to get to know him better, so that we could share something truly special... even if it probably wouldn't be for long, with him being a noble and all.

Gods, everything with Leo seemed so confusing.

His focus on having my "school" work was so strange. I'd never had anyone want something like that for me before. And he said he was going to make it happen, or at least try. What sort of man did that for a complete stranger? A good man. And even if I didn't know all of him, I loved that much of him in a warm and heartfelt way.

So... who did I want?

Could I really court all of them at the same time?

Would they agree?

"Tisi?"

The voice startled me. I'd been distracted again. I looked up to see...

"Kel? What are you doing here?"

He smiled. "I have a royal contract. I meet with generals, even the queen on occasion. It's not out of place for me to be in the royal palace."

"Right, yes, sorry. But... what are you doing... *here*?" I looked around. He was alone.

He checked for others too, then lowered his voice when he spoke. "I'm here for a royal advisory council meeting. They're held in the queen's private meeting chambers, not far from here. I was on my way there when I saw you." He looked at the door I guarded. "Is *she* here?"

I laughed. "Yes, *she* is." Then I realized just how easily we were talking. I'd even laughed at something he'd said.

"I... wanted to talk to you," he said softly.

A thrill ran through me. "I want to talk to you too." Both our voices were hushed now.

He drew close. If anyone else of his size had been this close to me, I might have been intimidated, but with Kel it just felt warm and comfortable. Without even touching me, I could feel his heat, smell his unique scent: leather and sweat, with a hint of lavender. As big and manly as he was, he enjoyed the scent of lavender and often had a touch of it in his bathwater.

I shivered at his nearness. My body responded as it had so long ago, when we'd coupled in the dark. Heat rose, filling me, even as it pooled into a molten puddle in my core. My breath quickened. My heart raced. Suddenly every shift of my blouse over my chest was like fire, every breath and beat of my heart rich with energy and life.

"I love you, Tisi. I never said it before, and I should have. I love you and even with all that's happened between us, I want to be with you. I want you back in my life." There it was. He'd said it plainly.

Oh, blessed Halea...

"I..." I did love him, and I wanted to say it, but my mouth didn't agree. My throat closed up. "I..."

Screw it.

I captured his head and brought it down as I rose up on my toes. My lips met his and suddenly everything was familiar and wonderful. All the passion I'd suppressed these past years overwhelmed me. A rather stunning desire gripped me, filled me with urgent need, spurred by the very likely possibility of being caught in this compromising position.

He lifted me easily, pressing my back to the wall. I wrapped my legs around his waist as our mouths opened and we tried to devour each other. My arms went around his neck, tight, pressing us close. My breasts crushed against his hard chest. The rough friction of fabric between us was almost painful against my aroused nipples.

I rocked my hips against him, feeling his arousal come alive even through our layers of clothes. One of his thick-fingered hands pushed between us and clamped over a breast, hard and kneading. I moaned into his mouth. Our times together had always been quick, and I was responding now as I had then, charging toward a hasty release.

I wanted him. I wanted this. I wanted our clothes to be off and have his thick cock inside me as he took me. It wouldn't take much, I was already primed and ready. Just a few hard thrusts while he pushed me up against this wall...

The wall...

In the palace.

Fuck!

I drew back quickly. "Not here!" I hissed as I unclamped my legs from around him and found the floor again, looking around.

No one had seen us. Yet that only meant I wanted to continue what we'd been doing.

But...

"Don't you have a meeting to get to?"

He looked around as well and captured me with a hard kiss before he stepped away. He didn't go far. "I do, but I have a bit of time and... I want you, Tisi," he whispered, his breath hot against my cheek as he pinned me to the wall again.

"I want you too," I said. Apparently, that was easier to say.

I needed to say more. Something about him not being the only one. But my mind was so clouded with heated desire for him that I couldn't quite recall those words either. Instead, I pulled him down for one last kiss, softly biting his lip.

With a quick check of the hall, no one around, he slid his hand down to bunch up my skirt and reach between my legs.

"Kel!" I hissed.

He grinned. "I'll keep an eye out. Just like old times."

And in some ways, it *was* just like old times: dangerous, a risk of being caught. But the danger of being found out was more of a thrill, not the life-threatening terror of the siege. Yet my body reacted the same: time was short, take pleasure where you can, and take it quick. And... Kel knew just how to touch me for maximum effect.

He pressed and flicked and rubbed. I quickly went from mostly-aroused to full-on soaking-wet and quivering. Then two of his thick fingers curled inside me as his thumb viciously massaged my clit. And when his other hand came up to mash against a breast, I came, biting my lip so as not to cry out, but feeling the full-body shudder of bliss flow through me.

Fuck me, but he was amazing! He'd always been able to get me off so fast with his fingers. He'd had to, to make sure his thick cock could slip inside me. But that didn't happen this time.

Kel withdrew his hand quickly and we adjusted ourselves, moving away from each other like nothing had happened.

But something *had* happened, and though it had been fast, it had been wonderful.

"What about you?" I whispered, still filled with the rush of that quick orgasm. "You deserve something."

"Later," he whispered. "When we can enjoy it, fully."

"I don't think we know what that's like," I joked.

He gave a soft laugh. "We'll find out."

And gods, how I wanted to find out. "I'll come to you," I said, hushed.

His grin was feral and his eyes full of heat. "Then we'll come together."

Oh, Hells yes, we would.

"I don't know if I can get away tonight, but tomorrow...?"

"I'll be waiting," he breathed. With a smile and a wink, Kel left.

It was only once he was gone and my mind slowly cleared of that heady lust-haze, that I recalled what I'd been supposed to say about rules and other guys.

"Fuck," I whispered.

Oh well. I'd see him again soon, and before we were together again, I'd tell him everything.

CHAPTER 23

TISERA

I GLOWED WITH PLEASANT WARMTH, VITAL, SEXY ENERGY thrumming through me. Yet Veora made no comment as we walked back to her house. She seemed distracted, lost in thought, which was good, because if she'd asked, I'd have spilled everything about what had happened with Kel at the palace.

It didn't feel real that he and I could be back together, even if I still had to talk to him about the *being with multiple guys* thing.

I'd do that eventually.

I floated back from Veora's house to mine. All my fatigue and worry from the previous night had vanished. I wanted to talk to Daz and enjoy one of his meals, to complete this wonderous day.

Then, on my way home, I encountered Leo. He was

on the road ahead of me, headed toward my place. Right. I had a lesson with him today.

And with him... were five young women. It seemed he *had* found some women to bring with him.

They walked ahead of me, facing away. I drew close behind them. "Leo?" I said, tentative, I didn't want to startle him.

He turned and his face lit up.

"Master Tisera! How nice to see you." And I couldn't miss how his eyes moved over me. I was dressed for my walks with Veora, which meant fancy and flirty. My bright, orange-gold silk blouse clung to my torso, form-fitting, with buttons down the front and billowing sleeves. The skirt was dark red, loose and long.

He usually saw me in my training clothes. And though he didn't say anything, I could tell from his surprised smile he didn't mind the different look.

"Let me introduce you to your new students." He motioned to the women with him. They too studied me with varying expressions: from skepticism to curiosity.

"Well," one of them piped up quickly. "We haven't agreed to do anything *yet*, just try it."

"I am a bit curious," another said. This one seemed bashful, blushing at the drop of a hat.

"Indeed," Leo said. He motioned to each in turn. "It is my pleasure to introduce Lady Willow Highcastle." This was the blushing one.

She curtseyed. She seemed young, though perhaps her constant semi-flushed state made her seem younger than she was. She had blond hair, so pale it seemed tinged with blue, and rich cobalt blue eyes. She wore a blue dress which set off her eyes.

"This is Lady Emarra Silvermoon." This was the first who'd spoken, seeming brash and a bit hot-blooded. She had strawberry blond hair and flashing forest green eyes. Her red dress was near to being scandalous, showing a little too much of her ample bosom, and the hem rose far above the ankle. She didn't curtsey, just glared at me.

Interesting.

The last three were: "Lady Sinda Rosewood, Lady Molli Merryweather, and Lady Hedra Featherwing." Of these, the first two were fairly standard nobles with blond hair and blue eyes, and the last, Hedra, had darker — more golden brown — hair and silvery-grey eyes.

I looked them over. The only one with any real mettle in her was Emarra. She might be a decent fighter one day, but then… that wasn't what I'd be training these women for. Leo had suggested more of a need for self-defense and protection. Certainly, all of them were pretty enough that they'd have no shortage of male attention, whether wanted or not.

So, I asked them.

"What do you want from this?" I held a hand up as Leo was about to answer. "I want to hear it from them." I turned to Emarra. I had a feeling if she agreed, the others would too. "You said you'd be up for trying it. I'm curious what you think *it* is?"

She clearly didn't like being put on the spot. She got defensive.

"All I know is Leo said we had to try training with you, that it would be useful and we'd get a lot out of it. He said you could teach us how to break the hands of any man who touches us the wrong way."

A very interesting way of putting it. Did they get "touched the wrong way" a lot?

Given their beauty, it wouldn't surprise me.

"I didn't used those words exactly," Leo cut in.

"It doesn't matter," I said to him. Then to Emarra. "Is that what you want? You're certainly quite attractive. You probably get a lot of attention from men. Would you like to know how to break a finger or two of those whose attention you *don't* want?"

She gave a grim smile. "That might be nice."

"I can teach you that right now. Consider it a free lesson, to get a taste for what I do."

Her eyes went wide. "Really? Now?" We were in the middle of a street, but traffic in this part of town was sporadic at this time of day.

I nodded, stepping in toward her. "Right now, yes." I put my hand on her chest. Her eyes went a little wider and she backed off.

"If a man wants to grope you, here's what you do. First, and this is the part that will surprise him and catch him off guard, capture his hand in both of yours — left hand over right hand — pressing his hand tight to you, as hard as you can." I stepped in again, placing my hand on her chest and nodded toward it.

Reluctantly, she captured my hand in both of hers, pressing hard. "This feels like I'd be encouraging him," she said.

"Don't worry, once you know how to do this, this part won't last too long," I said.

"Now... step back. With his hand captured and him wondering what you're doing he should be easy to pull off balance. It helps if you can crouch a little, get him to bend over."

She did so, and with my hand captured as it was, I had to follow her, stumbling forward. I caught myself, knowing that had been coming.

"Now, with your right hand, reach around my hand, get your fingers under it and twist it as you remove it from your chest, sandwich it in both hands, keep it tight."

She did so and saw how I was forced further in and down.

"Keep a firm hold with your right hand and release the left, press on my elbow, down."

She did and I was forced to the ground, kneeling.

"And now any man is at your mercy. You can break his fingers later, but for now, you've gotten his hand off you and with his hand locked up like this, you have control."

"Do I?" She forced me down a little further. She had a mean streak this one.

I grunted. "Trust me, you do. Now if you could please release me..."

She held a moment longer then released. I rose quickly shaking out my hand.

"What happened to your hand?" Emarra asked. I still had my knuckles bandaged from punching walls last night.

I gave a breathy laugh.

"If you really want to learn to fight, you have to accept the consequences, like some bloody knuckles now and then. It's not pretty, but trust me, it's worth the pain to be able to protect yourself." That wasn't the entire story, but I hoped it sounded good.

"Now. I want *you* to feel what I just did, so you know what it's like, how little strength you have once your hand is locked like that. Don't worry, I'll be gentle, but you need to be able to trust your own skills, know you can truly overpower nearly any man, so you have no hesitation."

Emarra was a tough one and wouldn't show 'weakness' in front of her little band of friends. "As you say." She drew herself up. "Shall I... touch you?" she asked.

I nodded.

She reached out. I was far quicker and more skilled, I grabbed her hand even before it hit my chest and gave it just a bit of a turn. She yelped, but after that, I slowed considerably and slowly forced her down, just a little. "Feel it?"

"Yes," she said, strained.

I released her instantly. "With practice, you'll learn to do it as quickly and easily as I just did."

She shook out her hand. "That was... amazing," she admitted reluctantly. "You moved so quickly!" Drawing herself up, she asked, "How much for a lesson?"

I looked at Leo. All of these women were probably stupidly wealthy, but they may not have access to funds quite as readily as a man might. I smiled when I said: "For men, I charge more, one strip of silver, but for women it's only a slip of silver per lesson."

Leo laughed. "That's a discount indeed." I couldn't tell if he was playfully upset or just trying to make it sound like a good deal.

Emarra nodded. "Seems fair. Shall we accompany Leo to his lesson now?"

I wanted a bit of time to prepare a lesson specifically for these women. "No, come again tomorrow, if that works?"

Emarra nodded curtly. "It does. I'll be there."

The other four all chimed in with some variation of "As will I."

"Do you want me back tomorrow, as well?" Leo asked.

I shrugged. I could teach him and these ladies at the same time. "Yeah, if you're feeling up to it."

"I'm sure I will be." He grinned.

We all walked just a bit farther down the road so I could show the ladies where I lived. Then the five young women left, whispering and giggling. One of them asked Emarra: "Can you teach me that?"

And that was that.

"I told you women would be interested," Leo whispered once the others were gone.

He had, and I was just a bit stunned.

"Will you teach me that move?" he asked.

"No, it's just for women. Unless you have a lot of people trying to fondle your chest?"

"Ah... no... but..." He flushed a little. Was he trying to be coy? If so, he was failing horribly, and it was adorable.

I wasn't sure what prompted me, perhaps the high of my super-hot encounter with Kel or the thrill of having more students, but I found words coming out of my mouth: "I wouldn't mind if you wanted to fondle *my* chest, though."

CHAPTER 24

TISERA

WHAT THE FUCK? HAD I JUST SAID THAT?

Leo blinked as we stared at each other.

He stepped in and pulled me close, his lips on mine. And where he may have been a beginner in combat, in this... he was no mere amateur. His lips were sure and soft, his hands encircling me, pressing us tight.

I hesitated, surprised for only an instant, before relaxing in his arms and opening my mouth to him. His tongue danced with mine as the kiss deepened. But then he stopped suddenly, pulling back.

A bit breathless and concerned, he asked, "Has Daz... your brother... talked to you?"

That was an odd question, especially given our current intimate state. "What?"

"Daz, has he talked to you about..." I could see Leo's

tension, he didn't want to say everything, but was hoping I'd understand.

I began to. "You know how Daz feels about me?"

He nodded. He released me a bit more, stepping back. "And if you know, then he has talked to you. I... I shouldn't..."

"You shouldn't what?" I was a bit thrown by this complete turnaround.

I could see he was trying to be chivalrous and gentlemanly. If I was another man's woman, then he wouldn't get in the way. But I didn't *belong* to any man, I never would. I would always be my own woman. Still, Leo's restraint was admirable and incredibly touching... and made me want him even more.

"Yes, I know how Daz feels, and I'm still coming to terms with that, but just because he loves me, doesn't mean I love him the same way. I don't know how I feel about him yet, but I do know how I feel about you, Leo. And right now, I want you to kiss me." I stepped in and quickly kissed him, to demonstrate.

Leo seemed stunned. "Oh... truly?"

"Yes," I breathed and kissed him again. "I'll figure out Daz later, right now I want you. Do you want me?"

"Yes," he breathed, close and heated.

I looked around. We were still close to where my laneway met the road, mostly out in the open. I grabbed Leo's hand and dragged him farther down the lane, then behind the thick trunk of one of the trees lining the drive, mostly out of sight of the road. I put my back to the tree and pulled him close, kissing him again, deep and needful.

His one hand slowly moved over the contours of my side and hip while the other slid into my hair, combing through the short-shorn locks.

A part of me insisted I should slow down, go over "the rules" or something, but it was a small part, so I ignored it. I didn't want to think about Kel or Daz or the rules, so I let myself indulge in the heated passion of this moment.

All I wanted to think about right now was Leo.

I cupped his cheek with one hand before sliding it up into his silken hair, pushing his lips harder to mine. I still had my bandages on, but I didn't care, and Leo didn't seem to either. My other hand went to his tight ass. He may not have been as big or imposing as Kel, but he was fit and firm and very insistent.

His one hand on my side came up to my breast. I moaned, feeling the sheer fabric move over my sensitive skin. He deftly unbuttoned several of the small ivory buttons and that same hand then slid under my shirt, his hot palm and caressing fingers hard on my breast as he moved his kisses off my lips to my chin, then my neck.

I'd been smoldering with heat since my time with Kel. Leo's insistence stirred those embers into a fire once again. We'd quickly progressed beyond kissing but I didn't care. My mind whirled with imaginings of what might happen: would Leo use those long dexterous fingers on me, as Kel had? Would there be more?

I wanted more.

Please let there be more.

I moved my hand from his tight rump to the front, lifting his doublet and undoing the silken tie on his pants. When my hand slipped under and in, I found his cock, hard and ready. Since the only other man I'd been with was Kel, I was quite surprised at the different feel of Leo's cock: long and slender, like the man himself. He wasn't as thick as Kel, but longer perhaps, smooth and firm in my grasp.

Leo didn't balk, didn't stop, didn't hesitate. My hand on his cock urged us well beyond kissing. He pressed kisses down over my neck and high onto my breasts. His hand, which had been wonderfully kneading my left breast, seized it, making me gasp. Then his lips descended to the taut nub of my nipple. He flicked his tongue over it, then gently raked his teeth along it, before capturing it in a lingering kiss.

His other hand moved down to my legs, bunching up my skirts. If he was startled by the daggers strapped to my thighs, he didn't show it. His nimble fingers slid over the rough hilt and leather sheathe, reaching higher, tracing in across my thighs. Then, his fingers brushed my folds and I gasped with the searing heat unleashed with his tentative touch.

"Yes," I breathed.

One of his long fingers found the hard nub of my clit. He circled it once, then flicked the sensitive bud. I clipped a cry, then bit my lip as he began pressing and rubbing wonderfully. I was already slick and slippery, and his attentions only made me more heated and wet.

Gods, we were doing this.

Heat sizzled through me, boiling my blood as my heart thundered. I was dizzy with expectant desire. My body shouted for more. I let myself be swept away by it.

I'd only imagined what it would be like with Leo

and… this hadn't been in any of my fantasies. I'd pictured us on a lush bed, with slow and sensual kisses, but this… This was like what I'd had with Kel at the palace, a driving and immediate need, an imperative to merge, hard and physical. I'd honestly thought Leo didn't have it in him.

I was pleasantly surprised, since this was more my speed anyway. Perhaps some other day we'd explore each other, slow and teasing. Today we were both bundles of tense desire, bursting with the fiery need to release.

My hand on his cock pulled hard letting him feel how much I wanted him. I was well past the point where a bit of fun fingering would do. I needed him inside me. His hand on my breast slipped away, down to my other thigh, hefting my skirt higher.

Then, surprisingly — since I wasn't sure he had the strength to lift a sturdy woman like me — he grabbed the underside of my thighs and boosted me up. My hand was pulled off his cock as I clamped my legs around his waist, helping to keep myself in place. This put my breasts at head level for him. He took my other nipple into his mouth, sucking insistently. I gasped at his attentions even as the tip of his slender cock brushed my wet folds.

I let out a long and unabashed moan of pleasure, then leaned down to whisper in his ear. "I want this. I want you, Leo." Just in case he had any hesitations about taking the next step.

He didn't.

Yet, where Kel might have thrust hard and entered me quickly, Leo played and teased, rocking his hips, wetting his tip in my folds first. Then, his thrusts ever so slowly deepened, each frisky push delving just a little deeper than the last.

And this drawn-out penetration — compared to what I'd known with Kel — drove me mad. I needed to feel his fullness. I gasped with the firm press of each teasing touch on my extremely receptive and responsive opening.

"Enough play," I hissed and tightened my legs around him pulling my hips down over him, driving him deep inside me. He may not have been as thick as Kel, but that didn't stop me from feeling every glorious inch of him. I let out a long moan of near-orgasmic revelation at the press of his erection deep inside me. He added short thrusts to my movements, pounding my clit when we met.

His lips slipped off my nipple — now very aroused — and I gasped. Then he tilted his head back, and I lowered my lips to his. Our mouths pressed, wet and deep, as he drove me to the brink of bliss.

Gods, I wanted this so bad. I'd been blissfully buzzed, worked up by Kel earlier. It wouldn't take much to get me off. Leo's thrusts quickened. Our faces drew apart as we gasped and groaned. Our gazes locked, hot and intense. His sea-green eyes blazed with desire.

"Come," I whispered. "Come with me." Then I couldn't speak as I was thrown over the brink of bliss into the yawning chasm of a hot and pounding orgasm.

Leo drove himself hard within me one final time, his cock pulsing with his release. Heat bloomed inside me. He whispered a soft but insistent: "Yes!"

I clasped myself around his shaft, hard, wanting to

feel every throbbing pulse, and that only intensified his experience. His eyes widened as he gasped.

"Gods," he breathed.

I found enough breath to whisper: "They had nothing to do with it."

He laughed. And that caused both of us to lose our breath again as the mirthful convulsions threw us back into waves of ecstasy. And when that subsided, Leo pulled me close into his arms, holding me as we slowly regained our breath.

"Wow," I breathed, next to his ear. I could still feel the pulse and surge of his release within me, relentless. Occasionally he'd shudder and hold me closer. I'd never felt so intimate with someone, so cherished and needed and sexy.

When he did eventually finish, our bodies starting to cool, we slowly disengaged, and he let me down.

"I'm sorry if that was too quick and abrupt," Leo said softly.

"That was fucking amazing, is what it was," I gasped, flushed and still a little breathless, mouth dry. "We couldn't have done slow if we'd wanted to. We'll do slow... later."

Would he want to be with me again, or had this been a once-only thing?

Those sea-green eyes caught mine in a long and loving glance. "Tisi..." He blinked as his brow furrowed. "Can I call you that?"

"Yes," I whispered, with a breath of a laugh. After what we'd just done, he could call me whatever he wanted.

"I... I should tell you, I cannot court you. I cannot offer you everything a man should offer you. I can flirt and play... if you like... but..."

"Oh, Leo," I breathed relieved. "I'm so glad you said it. I don't want anything serious. All I wanted was some fun with you, your passion and warmth. I know it can't really last. You're a noble, and I'm not."

"Oh." He blinked, then a grin slowly spread on his face. "Ohhhh."

"Exactly." We had both wanted the same thing yet not been certain the other wanted it.

"And what about our lessons?" he asked. "You're my instructor."

"And now I'm your lover. I'm talented, I can be both."

He smiled at that. "Yes. Yes, you can... can't you?" He laughed a bit. "You can do anything."

I wasn't sure exactly what that meant, but I liked the sound of it.

"I—" Words fled me as I happened to glance over Leo's shoulder and see... Daz. He was some distance down the lane, but he'd seen... everything. "Fuck!"

"What?" Leo blinked, startled.

"Sorry, Leo I... have to go." I pressed a finger to his lips to stop any argument. I locked eyes with him again. "Leo, that was amazing and I definitely want to do that again, as well as continue our lessons, but I... just remembered something I need to do. We should talk... about all of this, but can we do that... later?"

He seemed a bit taken aback by my sudden bluntness but then smiled and nodded. "Anything for you, Tisi, anything."

Gods, he was amazing. He gave so freely, understood everything, followed my instructions, and asked so little in return. I didn't deserve a man like him. I wasn't sure how I'd gotten him, but right now... he wasn't the man I really needed to talk to.

"What about our lesson today?" he asked quickly.

"We both just learned something very valuable. Can we leave it at that? We'll continue our regular lessons tomorrow, if that's acceptable?"

"Yes."

So accepting and unquestioning. I kissed Leo again then smiled.

"Thanks, you're amazing, I have to run!" And I did, hiking my skirts to run down the lane to the house.

I honestly didn't know what I was going to say to Daz.

...I just hoped, I hadn't lost him... forever.

CHAPTER 25

Tisera

"Daz?" I called as I burst through the door of the cottage.

The main room was quiet, unoccupied. The door to his room was closed. I ran over and opened it. He hadn't locked it. He sat on the side of his bed, head in his hands.

"Daz—" but what could I say? *That wasn't what it looked like*? It had been exactly what it looked like, and I had enjoyed it and very much wanted to do it again. So, what then?

Then... as had happened with Leo, words spilled out before I'd fully thought about them. "I love you!"

What?

Fuck! Really?

Did I?

Well, yes, definitely in one sense, but in the way *he* wanted...?

He looked up, eyes red-rimmed, tears on his cheeks. "How can you say that?" His voice broke, raw and hoarse.

How could I? I wasn't exactly sure, but I knew one thing, "What you saw, me and Leo, that wasn't love." It had been raw and hot and immediate. Gods, it had been great sex, but not really love, I was sure of that.

He sniffed. "How can you love me and still fuck him?"

That... was more complicated.

"I... had wanted to talk to you, about what you'd said yesterday, but then... what happened with Leo... just happened. I still need to talk to you, and make sense of everything I'm feeling, but none of this is working out like I thought it would."

"None of this? None of... what?" He sighed heavily. "You want to talk. Talk, but I can see your aura. It's all yellow and orange and sienna right now... LOTS of sienna!"

I didn't know what that meant. "Is that bad?"

"It means you're very aroused and blissful and excited. I can *see* the results of what you were just doing, Dizzy. It's..." His jaw tightened and twitched. He looked away.

"Oh... sorry." I didn't know how to respond to that. "Can you see that I want to be honest with you right now? That it's the truth when I say that was something I didn't mean to happen and that I do... love you? Can you see that?"

Gods, I hoped that was the truth. I didn't know what he could see with his emotion-color-sense-thingy.

He faced me again. His jaw tensed. He seemed angry. He shook his head. "I don't know how that can be true, but I can see it. Your blue is strengthening. I'll be keeping an eye on that as you talk, so... talk."

Blue? Blue was honesty? Interesting.

He shook his head, as if what he saw didn't make any sense to him. He couldn't believe it, not yet.

I closed the door and leaned against it with a heavy sigh. How... how did I say this? I tried to recall Veora's words but couldn't.

Time to say it my way.

"I... I want to have a different relationship with you Daz. I'm... exploring many facets of myself right now, and apparently there are several men — well, three men including you — interested in me. Leo is one of them. I... I don't know who I want to be with yet, but I'd like to explore a relationship with all of you. I'm glad you were honest with me and said what you did. It's taken me a while, but I've begun to see you in a different way as well. I'd like to explore that with you, if you're willing, but you have to know I'll be exploring it with others at the same time. If... if you really want me to be happy and find a true and perfect love in my life, then hopefully you'll let this happen and perhaps that love will be with you."

Daz looked confused. "You want to... be with three men... at the same time?"

I got a little defensive. "It's not like most men don't fool around with lots of women before finding the one they'll settle down with. Why can't a woman?"

Daz's expression hardened. "I'm not like that. I've never been like that. I've always known you were the only one for me."

Oh. Right.

"Well, I love you, Daz. I love you as I've always loved you, and I can see the potential to love you in a different way as well. But it's going to take some time for me to adjust. I had hoped we'd do that together."

"While you're fucking other guys?" Bitterness poured out of his words.

"Ah... well, yes." I had to be honest. "But you see, that's the whole point!"

"To fuck other guys?" He was wide-eyed, incredulous.

"No, listen. With Leo and—" Fuck, say it, be honest, "—with Kel, I—"

"You're back with Kel?"

"He's the third man, yes. We talked recently and found out all our anger and resentment came from a massive misunderstanding. We're going to try being together again, but *listen* Daz, this is important!"

His jaw twitched, perhaps from keeping it so tightly closed, but he nodded.

"With Kel, all I ever had was a physical relationship, nothing more. There really wasn't any love." We'd only just been getting to that point when we'd made our mistakes and shattered our chances.

"And with Leo, well that's complicated. And what happened today is only going to make it more complicated. But with him as well, it was a mostly physical thing. With Leo and Kel, what I'll need to explore is less about sex and more about what you've always been to me, which is a companion who's there for me in other ways. That won't be easy."

Perhaps I could stroke his ego just a little? "In that domain you're way ahead of them. You're my rock, Daz, my constant companion, the one I depend on for... everything!"

I drew in a long breath and tried to let out all the tension I was holding. I went to him and knelt, hands on his knees.

"Daz, I don't need to explore that with you. I know I can count on you to be a dependable partner. I already love that part of you." I lowered my voice a little, breathy and inviting. "Daz, what I need to explore with you is sex; lots and lots of amazing sex." I mocked a sigh. "If you're not up for that..."

I held his gaze, those caramel brown eyes wary.

"Am I still blue?" I asked.

His voice was just a little choked up in an odd way when he said, "Yes."

"So, I'm telling the truth, aren't I?"

"Yes," he said, again strained and tight.

"That I want to have lots of sex with you. Heaps of hot, steamy, gasping, groping, wet and—"

He made a gasping, coughing sound, turning a remarkable shade of crimson.

"So... what do you say?"

We silently gazed at each other for a long time as he considered, still red-faced and practically vibrating. I could see how desperately he wanted to be with me. It was practically bursting out of him. Hopefully, I'd quelled his reservations about the others.

And... I did want to be with him.

Looking up at him now, that chiseled, ruddy face, those deep, soft caramel eyes. He was a dear friend, so very close to my heart. Definitely handsome, but was he sexy?

I tried to picture him naked. I hadn't seen him fully unclothed in a while, so I had to guess at some bits, but I had a good imagination and I pictured him tall, proud, and ready. Oh! Well, it seemed he could be very sexy, in my imagination at least.

He swallowed heavily before saying. "Your sienna is rising again."

"That's my arousal, right?" I smiled. My fantasy had gotten me feeling warm and ready to be with this amazing man who'd always been there for me when I'd had no one else.

"Yes," he said and quickly leaned down to kiss me. It wasn't a long kiss, and he drew back looking me over again. "Is that... for me?"

"It is," I said. And I meant it.

He shuddered. "By Evos," he breathed. He grabbed my arms and pulled me up to him. His next kiss was not so quick.

CHAPTER 26

T<small>ISERA</small>

I <small>DREW BACK FROM THAT LONG AND BREATH-STEALING KISS</small>, and shuddered as a thrill went down my spine.

"How do you want me?" I whispered. I shifted, kneeling between his legs, and began undoing the tie on his pants.

He gently pushed my hands away, capturing them together between his. Only then did he seem to notice the bandages. "What... happened?"

I breathed a laugh. "I was... confused and frustrated last night. Punching walls seemed like a good idea. Not so much now, though."

He shook his head slowly and began undoing the bandages. He unwrapped one hand and clasped it between his own. The warmth of his healing flowed into me. The pain vanished. Then he tended to the other hand.

"Doesn't this tire you?" I said, concerned.

He shook his head again with a faint smile. "These wounds were superficial, minor. Healing them won't hinder me much for what is to come."

"And what *is* to come?" I asked, breathy, curious. His healing warmth on my hands had only made the rest of me even more heated and ready.

"I want to show you how much you mean to me." Those caramel eyes captured me in an intense and loving look. "I want to give you something I don't think you've ever had before, Dizzy. I want to give you *all* my love."

I wasn't sure what that meant, but I had the feeling I'd soon find out. He reached up, placing his hand beside my head. He wasn't touching me but was so close I could feel the heat of his hand on my temple. He made a stroking motion, as if smoothing my wild hair, moving down to my cheek and I felt it, not his hand, but something... more!

It was like raw power, but soft and gentle. A caress on my skin with thrills of something so pure and penetrating it resonated in my very soul.

I gasped and shuddered at the intensity of it.

"That... was pure red," he whispered. "The essence of love and strength." He smiled tenderly.

This intense essence, this power permeating and filling my being... *this* was his love?

Wow. It was pure and powerful, so profound that tears leaked from my eyes as I sat there, overwhelmed.

"Have I ever told you your aura is dazzling?" he whispered. "Even when you're just resting, being yourself, you are nearly all red, a being of radiant power, beautiful and dangerous and intoxicating."

His fingers brushed my face, and that same power surged through his touch. I was helpless in its sway, as love — like none I had ever known — filled me.

"This is what I feel for you," he said. His words were quiet and sincere, but the implications, the power, left me stunned and speechless.

It was beautiful and potent and perfect.

And when he bent down and kissed me, his full lips to mine, it lifted me, not just emotionally, but...physically. He stood slowly and I rose with him, pulled to my feet — then *off* my feet — by the power of his aura. He embraced me as his lips left mine. I floated, weightless in his arms.

He smiled, a soft and secret thing I'd never seen before.

He whispered, "I'm going to take my time. I've been dreaming of this for years. I want it to be perfect. All you have to do... is feel my love."

"Yes, I will," I breathed. It wasn't like me to give up control, but carried by his love and power, I was curious what sex could be like when it was more than just physical and quick.

I relaxed in his arms, still light as air and buoyant as he kissed my cheeks, then ears, then neck and shoulders. I hadn't really done up my shirt after the romp with Leo, so it was easy for him to push it to one side as he pressed kisses to my shoulders. Each brush of his lips on my skin bloomed with warmth and devotion.

He undid the few remaining buttons and the silken shirt fluttered to the floor. Daz took his precious time kissing lower still, each press filling me with the purity of his love, a warmth so very different from the heat of desire.

Still, my passion and arousal were whipped up within me, thrumming through me, hot and surging with every hammering beat of my heart. Yet it remained secondary to the pureness of adoration which Daz infused within me.

And when his lips pressed gently to the swelling bud of a nipple, he trembled. Hot breath escaped his lips as he gasped. Something about that heated exhalation thrilled straight from my nipple out to every part of me, so intense I could only let out a strange gasping breath of my own, unable to make a sound.

Something visceral, a humid desire flooded my chest. It took me a moment to realize... it had come from Daz. He'd added his lust and longing to the love coursing through me.

It swelled within me, turning the liquid heat of my passion to blazing flames, filling me to my fingers and toes, and the top of my head. I shook with tremors of searing desire from that one kiss. And when he kissed my other — now hard as Hells — nipple even more desire poured into me. I let out an unabashedly loud moan as his passion — and mine — threatened to consume me.

His kisses moved down over my abdomen as his hands moved to my skirt, undoing the ties and pushing it off. I trembled as the silk slid over my buttocks, then whispered by my legs.

He knelt and kissed my belly and hips, then over the tops of my thighs and in...

I opened my legs, finding them weightless like the rest of me. Since he no longer held me, I found I could move freely in this strange floating state. I laid back, giving Daz better access to me.

The soft press of his lips to my already slick opening made me gasp. Then came the most miraculous sensation, like he was inside me, moving, full and deep. A gentle thrusting of power, not just filling my folds but *all* of me.

That throbbing power infused me with near-delirious elation.

Daz found my clit and gave it a lick with his tongue before pressing his lips over me and sucking lightly. The fullness within me heaved and thrusted like some miracle cock, until I was on the verge of a mind-blowing orgasm. Then it swelled, and I cried out as I was filled with an ecstasy so powerful, I couldn't contain it. I erupted with a release so powerful it overwhelmed all my senses.

But it was a spiritual thing, allowing me to remain at that mind-shattering apex, experiencing it over and over. His powers held me in sway. I was at his mercy, lost in this extremity of bliss.

Then, his tongue pushed into my folds, and I opened to him. A physical release blasted through me, adding to the spiritual one. It was *by far* the most potent orgasm I'd ever known. His power and love were the pendulous clapper, and I was the bell, being rung, over and over, loud and joyous and resonant.

Every part of me tensed then released in a series of

fierce waves, which left me filled with hazy, glorious, serene bliss.

Every thrashing beat of my heart sent a new pulse of rapturous joy through me.

I screamed — probably a lot — but I was too lost in this place of pure and radiant ecstasy to care.

Time passed. I came to myself slowly.

I lay on a soft surface... a bed.

A heated body pressed to mine, skin to skin. It took me a moment to remember who this was: Daz.

Wonderful, amazing, miraculous Daz.

He traced his fingers over my skin, leaving a trail of pleasant, tingling heat where they passed.

My eyes fluttered open. Lying beside me, propped on one arm, was the smiling face of the man I loved.

And I did love him. I loved him in all possible ways. He'd shown me how much he loved me and it had been beyond description.

I wanted more of that... *all the time*!

I smiled, then tried to speak, but my voice was raw, my throat parched.

He laughed a little. "You were... very vocal about that first round," he whispered.

Removing the hand which had been tracing lines on me, he reached over me to his nightstand, picking up a pitcher of water, pouring some into a cup, which he gave to me.

"Here," he said. "Drink."

I sat up and took the cup in both hands to drain it.

Elevated as I was, I could see both of us. Sometime, while I'd been insensate, he'd removed his clothes. We lay together, naked. I wasn't a "precious, pale beauty" like some women. I enjoyed the sun and was well tanned. Still, Dazar's soft brown skin made mine look pale in comparison.

The water was cool and refreshing, and I cleared my throat, testing it. "That was amazing," I whispered. "And... you didn't even come, did you?"

"Not yet, no."

"Is that what comes next, your pleasure?" I asked. His cock twitched and grew as he considered that.

"No. Next is more for you. I get mine once you've been *thoroughly* pleasured."

I laughed. "You were *very* thorough the first time." But I wouldn't turn down *more* of that indescribable pleasure.

I put the cup down and leaned over to kiss him lightly before laying back again. I whispered, "I'm all yours, do your worst."

"Oh... I will," he said, leaning down to kiss high on my chest. And from that kiss the wonderful warmth of his love spread through me again.

"Ohhhh!" I breathed softly.

When he lifted away, he whispered, "Do you trust me?"

"Yes, always," I breathed.

"You have always been deeply in control of every part of yourself and your life. I want to give you a moment where you don't need to worry, don't need your walls up, don't need to be strong. Just... let go and enjoy and feel."

As he said this, he made a swirling motion with his hand and both my arms raised up from my sides. They moved up and over my head to lay on the bed, one wrist over the other. They weren't bound, but they felt as if they were. I didn't mind at all. He wouldn't hurt me, quite the contrary, and the position, so open, thrusting up my chest, so vulnerable to... attack... sent a new thrill through me.

"I'm all yours," I whispered.

I didn't think anything could surprise me after that first round of miracle sex.

I was wrong.

CHAPTER 27

TISERA

DAZ LEANED OVER AND KISSED ME, SOFTLY AT FIRST. Slowly we opened our lips to each other as he showed me the fullness of his passion in that one lingering, deep kiss.

Then... he seemed to split. He lifted away, but an afterimage of him remained, still kissing me, lips pressed to mine.

It was curious and strange, but I didn't question it. Daz was powerful and mystical, and if he could be kissing me and doing other things at the same time, something told me I wasn't going to mind too much.

The second Daz slid his hand up my side to a breast, pushing up the responsive swell as he brought a second set of lips down upon it. He kissed it then took it into his mouth, sucking while running his tongue around the sensitive nub.

Again, a fragment of him moved away while one

remained. His hand and lips still caressed and stimulated one breast while the third Daz moved to the other side. A third set of lips brought me to dual, nipple-standing arousal and remained there, while yet another Daz moved on!

More and more of him appeared, lips kissing, hands pressing and caressing and I was beginning to wonder why I didn't have multiple men tend to me *all* the time.

This was absolutely amazing!

I relaxed into his caresses, letting him stimulate every inch of my oh-so-sensitive skin.

When he sought my folds, I felt not only his kissing lips and the slip of his tongue, but the press and probe of his fingers, not just from one hand, but *both*. All of it, impossibly in the same place at once, working in tandem to stimulate me beyond reason.

I couldn't quite tell when blistering pleasure finally peaked into a prolonged orgasm. My bliss didn't spike, so much as it expanded to encompass all of me, thrumming through my body and filling my spirit with heavenly delight.

I moaned and mumbled as elation washed over me like waves on a beach. And the tide was coming in, those waves growing ever more powerful as my pleasure only seemed to build.

And when the second — far more powerful — orgasm hit, I cried out, writhing and squirming in uncontrollable ecstasy. But even then, *it didn't stop*.

My cries turned to tremulous, gasping breaths and between them I begged.

"Please," I whispered. "Please, please, please!" It became my mantra.

"Yes?" The hot breath of my lover on my ear sent a new thrill through me.

"Please, fuck me! I want to feel you. I want you to come. I need you! Please!" I'd never begged for a man before, never been this open and vulnerable and vocal.

In the next instant the many mystical Daz's faded back to one, still lying beside me. I was left panting and tingling as I lay amidst the exquisite bliss of that last powerful release.

Daz rose and shifted, moving between my legs. I opened myself to him as he knelt low. Then he grabbed my thighs and pulled me down to him. I yelped with the movement, a gleeful, playful noise, knowing I'd receive what I'd asked for very soon.

I looked down at the proud tower of his erection, throbbing and hard. His cock was robust and tall, with a heavy, flared tip. I couldn't wait to see what he could do with it.

He bent over me, kissing one taut nipple. One of his arms slid under my butt, lifting me, as his other hand made sure his cock found my folds.

I was so very aroused and ready for him after everything he'd done. When he pressed and pushed inside me, we both gasped with impassioned surprise. He stopped there, his gloriously large tip pressing wonderfully against me. I wriggled around, teasing his cock with my writhing hips, and loving how he felt, rolling around inside me. Daz smiled as he pulled up and away from my breasts, kneeling straight.

Then he grabbed my hips, bracing me as he drove his cock deep into me.

I cried out with bliss, wrapping my legs around him.

He rolled his hips, thrusting with each motion. He pressed a hand down over my curls, his thumb slipping down to stroke my clit in time with his thrusts.

Given everything he'd already done, that was more than enough to whip me into a third body-clenching orgasm. I clamped down on him, hard, milking his cock, wanting him to come... but he only grinned down at me and whispered, "Not yet."

I wanted to beg him to come, but I couldn't speak. That last release had stolen my voice and nearly all of my breath. Instead, I spoke with my body, bucking and writhing around his cock as best I could, hoping to tease a release out of him. But he remained strong and hard inside me.

"No," he whispered. I barely heard his words through my haze of bliss. "Other men have taken you here. I wish for my first time with you to be a first for you as well."

I had no clue what he meant by this, but I didn't care. After all he'd given me, he could do whatever he liked.

"Do you trust me?" he whispered again.

I nodded.

He moved us, shifting slowly and carefully. He withdrew as I was repositioned on my hands and knees, with him behind me. Then came pressure on my rear entrance and only then did I understand what he'd meant.

Exhilaration thrilled through me.

I'd never been one to shy away from trying new things. I managed to moan a soft "yes," to encourage him.

He whispered something and slid into me with ease. I would have thought I'd be tight. Perhaps he'd used his powers on me? I didn't really care because he felt massive and marvelous inside of me.

I let out a series of cries as he pushed in deeper. I kept thinking he couldn't possibly go farther, only to feel him fill me even more.

And when my cheeks finally pressed to his loins, I'd become a whimpering mess: trembling with need. This newfound place of pleasure rocked me with waves of bliss as I neared yet another orgasm.

His hands moved down my flanks and prompted me up, helping me kneel in front of him. My back pressed to the round, hard muscles of his chest as one of his arms rose to a breast, kneading it roughly. His other hand slid down to find my clit and began a rhythmic stroking in time with his thrusts from behind. I put a hand over each of his, urging him, pressing harder, feeling his need finally matching my own.

"Yes," I whispered again, I could feel it, his mounting pleasure, the heave and swell of his cock, the quickening pace as he grunted and pushed and drove himself to his release. My passion rose with his.

Higher.

Higher!

He let out a roar, slamming himself deep within me. The throbbing surge of his release bloomed inside me, driving me to a final, body-throbbing orgasm as I came with him.

A massive swell of orgasmic pleasure — not my own — enveloped me. Given everything else he'd done, I guessed this was Daz's bliss — the pure euphoric rapture of his release — transferred from his aura to mine.

It was too much.

Far too much!

I joined his roaring shout as my release became a flood so powerful it surged between the fingers of Daz's hand and mine, pressed to my folds.

I laughed, too lost to euphoria to care.

He grunted as I must have contracted around him. Still connected to his aura, I felt that spike of bliss too... which caused even more of a mess.

We collapsed onto the bed both panting and laughing in turns, wet and messy, but feeling so wonderfully connected and overjoyed.

"You're going to need a new bed," I said through my giggles.

"I'll sleep in yours," he whispered, kissing my back, arms wrapped tight around me.

I'd never just slept with a man before, but after everything Daz had done — how amazing this time with him had been — I figured I could allow him to share my bed.

Yet we were so exhausted we fell asleep in his.

We woke late in the evening. With the long summer's days, it was still twilight out. Daz became his domestic-god self and went to make some dinner. I slipped on a robe and went for a quick bath. The waters were still tepid after the heat of the day. I quickly washed myself, feeling refreshed and full of life.

I lingered in the bath after I'd washed, even though the waters grew colder. I needed a moment to collect my thoughts.

Mostly... I wondered why in the blazes of the Five Hells, I hadn't done this sooner! Why had I kept myself so guarded, not putting myself out there for this amazing love?

The answer to that came quickly: I'd kept my walls up... because of Kel. He'd hurt me so badly — torn my heart out — and I'd not wanted anything from any man. Despite all my fearlessness in battle, I'd been terrified of being hurt in love again.

But that had been a horrible misunderstanding. Kel loved me.

And Leo loved me...

And Daz loved me.

Could Kell give me the same slow and sensual experience I'd just had with Daz? He didn't have the same magical powers to touch my aura and stimulate me that way, but still... could he be attentive and loving and slow? I actually didn't know, but I wanted to find out.

And even though my experience with Leo had been hot and quick, I was certain he could be every inch the gentleman in bed, and love me like some fancy noble-lady, showered in roses and kisses, seeking only my lasting pleasure before he joined with me.

Despite the cooling water, I was getting quite hot.

I had three men who wanted me, but... who did *I* want?

I wasn't sure where it came from, but my mind latched onto the heady fantasy of *all three* men pleasuring me, driving me crazy with their heated lust and abiding love.

Kel in front, thick and hard inside me.

Daz behind, thrusting as he had that afternoon.

Leo kissed and caressed, needing nothing for himself as he sought only my pleasure.

And the combined bliss was unimaginable.

But it was truly a fantasy.

Those three men couldn't be more different. There was no way they'd ever be together like that.

Which led back to the question still haunting me: Which one did I want?

And the niggling answer, which whispered: *all of them.*

CHAPTER 28

Tisera

THE NEXT DAY, WHILE I ESCORTED VEORA TO THE PALACE, I told her about my encounters with the guys the day before. I found myself growing giddy, a silly smile on my face, which I couldn't hide and didn't want to.

"Oh, wow," she breathed. "It sounds like you fully embraced my advice and went for it. Though, for Leo and Kel, you still need to tell them you want to see them *and* others at the same time. Or..." Her tone grew mischievous. "You don't *have* to. It's not like men don't do it all the time, being with multiple women, cheating on their wives and lovers with others. Usually those situations end badly, though, and I get the sense you care too much for each of these men to wish for that?"

"Indeed," I said, not able to imagine trying to keep all those relationships secret. "If I'm going to do this, they all need to know the truth." To myself I then whispered, "I hope they can handle it."

"Oh, it sounds like you're really in trouble, Tisi," Veora said lightly. "You want to be with all of them all of the time, don't you?"

I had to admit it: "I do... is that even possible?"

Veora sighed.

"There are tribes in the far north, beyond the Valterran Mountains, who live in family groups with several husbands and several wives. They have complex relationships, but they never stray outside of their family. Even the Dathi have been known to share mates, occasionally. It isn't common for them, but occasionally a man will have two wives or a woman two husbands, though rarely more than two. If you want all three, you'll be starting something entirely new, at least here in Pearlia."

"I shouldn't even think of it," I whispered. "The more I do, the more I want it, but as you say, it's not likely to happen. I... I feel like I'm going to hurt someone eventually, maybe all of them. But I don't want to hurt any of them."

What a horrible — and wonderful — situation I'd gotten myself into.

"Then the best advice I can give is enjoy it while it lasts. Hopefully, you'll end up with at least one of them, and hopefully it's the right one. But in the meantime—" she lowered her voice to a conspiratorial tone, "—fuck all three and enjoy every moment of it!"

I was a bit surprised at her language — she was a lady after all — but she winked at me, and I laughed.

I decided I'd take her advice and enjoy this curious time in my life. I was healthy, there were no wars, and I had three men who loved me. *And* I was finally in a place where I wanted them to love me.

I shivered just a little with the anticipation of my next encounter, though I reminded myself that if it was with Kel or Leo, they needed to know the rules first. No more leading them on.

I'd told Kel I'd see him tonight... but I also had a lesson with Leo this afternoon. And our lessons would no longer be private. I had to remember that. Gods, I was so flustered and excited all at the same time.

Veora and I chatted like dearest friends. She gave me some tips for how to please men, some of which I'd known about but not yet tried, others were... new — and a bit shocking — to me. But I drank it all in.

Once we were at the palace, we proceeded up through the servant's halls to the prince's room, where I dropped her off.

I stayed on guard and tried *not* to think about how I might use Veora's lascivious suggestions on each of my glorious guys.

I needed to remain focused.

And in my state of heightened alertness, I caught the sound of fighting, distant but unmistakable. I rushed to a nearby window, which looked out over the palace's yard.

Below me was a sight I'd never seen in the palace: men fighting and dying. This was no mock combat, no training or practice. This was true battle.

A large covered wagon disgorged armed men who

spread out into the palace, slaughtering guards as they went. The cobblestones were bathed in blood.

I blinked, not fully understanding what I was seeing.

The palace was being attacked...

And I needed to do something about it.

CHAPTER 29

Tisera

I sprinted back to the prince's quarters and barged into the suite, then into his bedchambers. I halted at the sight of the carnal act before me. Veora straddled the prince, sitting proud as she rocked herself over him. Her hands combed up through her hair, head thrown back. The prince's hands clutched her — very well endowed — breasts as he drank in her beauty. Then he looked at me, a little shocked.

"The palace is under attack!" I hissed at them. "I'll protect you, but you should bar your door and find cover!"

That stopped them both, and since I didn't want to see any more than I already had, I left, returning to the hall.

If the attackers got this far, I'd have no cover along

this open hallway. If they had any crossbows with them, I'd be an easy target. Which meant I'd want to be at one end of the long hall or the other, either to attack them up close as soon as they turned the corner or be able to use that corner as cover if they were coming from the other direction... but that would mean leaving the prince's door unprotected and I couldn't do that. I had to stay here, out in the open.

To make matters worse, I was dressed as a commoner, not a soldier. I reached under my skirts and drew forth the two long daggers strapped to my thighs.

What I wouldn't give for a sword and shield, but this was all I had, and it would have to do. If I was lucky, I could take a sword from one of the attackers.

But then I realized something... the fact that I was dressed as a commoner could be used to my advantage. I flipped both daggers, holding them reversed so they were almost completely hidden behind my arms. If anyone saw me — including the attackers — they'd not think me a threat. They might get close without trying to harm me... then I could take them.

With luck, though, the attackers wouldn't even get this far. I was deep in the royal wing of the palace. It was highly unlikely that—

Was that the sound of fighting?

Fuck.

I heard the clank of metal and the thud of heavy booted feet from one direction and turned to see — thankfully — a troop of four palace guards coming around a corner, jogging urgently toward me.

"What are you doing out here?" one called to me. "Find cover, they're in the royal wing!"

I nodded but didn't move. Hopefully they'd think I was some silly, scared-stiff, courtier or servant.

They ran past me to the far corner of the hall, where the sounds of fighting drew closer. They waited at the corner, then charged around in a rush.

More sounds of combat, mixed with the groans and screams of dying men.

Someone staggered into view around the corner: a palace guard. He looked disbelieving at the crossbow bolt sticking out of his stomach. He collapsed to his hands and knees and looked up at me.

"Run!" he wheezed, then collapsed.

I cowered, crouching low, as more men came into view. These were not palace guards, and the amount of other-people's blood on them told me they were hardened mercenaries, very skilled at close quarter combat. There were seven of them, some injured. Two men with crossbows hurried to the front.

One man spied me and laughed. "Look at the pretty lass, Sergeant. You sure I can't have a little fun?"

"No, our orders are clear, kill her."

Dear gods! Their orders were to kill everyone? Even civilians? What sort of inhuman commander did they have?

"No!" I yelped, and it wasn't entirely feigned. I'd have much preferred if the cocky one had tried something with me, gotten close with no weapons out. It would have been easier to kill him that way. But now...

Luckily the men with the crossbows didn't want to

waste ammunition on me, since I'd be easy prey for one of their mates with a sword. They passed me as if I was no threat to them. One of the others approached, sword out.

"Sorry lass," this one said. "I'd much rather stab you with a different sword, but orders is orders." He drew back his sword, ready to stab me through the chest, quick and mostly clean.

I surged to my feet, meeting his blade with a dagger and pushing it aside. Then I slit the wrist of his sword hand with my other dagger. Dropping one dagger, I plucked the man's sword from a now lifeless grip, then swung it up across his neck. Yet I was a bit too eager, my aim too high, cleaving through his jaw, but it had the same effect.

He was dead before he hit the ground.

"Fuck me, she killed Petric!" one shouted.

I couldn't afford to stop. I had six others to kill, and I wasn't in armor. I had to trust in speed and surprise. And surprise wouldn't last long.

I charged a second man and stabbed for his throat. He shook off his shock and raised his sword to parry mine, but he wasn't expecting the dagger I drove into the unprotected spot under his right arm. The long-bladed dagger plunged deep and he fell, dying.

Knowing there might be attacks coming my way from behind, I threw myself down, diving and rolling. I came up kneeling at the back of the group, where one of the injured men swung at me awkwardly with a sword in his left hand — clearly not his usual sword arm.

I blocked the clumsy blow with my dagger and drove my sword up, trying to get under the faulds of his armor and hopefully slice into his belly. But the blade deflected awkwardly and tore into his codpiece, my sword sinking into his soft and precious parts.

The man screamed and dropped his sword to clutch his bloody loins. I took that moment to surge to my feet and slice my dagger across his throat.

Another injured man — clutching a wound on his side with one hand — lunged at me. I twisted — unable to get fully out of the way in time — and took the hit on my hip, instead of my stomach. The blade glanced off my hipbone, scraping and biting deep.

I cried out at the searing pain, even as I slashed wildly at him. My sword rang off his helm. He staggered, stunned. I surged in and punched him with my sword-hand, smashing the cross-guard of the blade into his nose. He gave a gurgling cry and fell back, clutching his ruined face. He might die, he might live, but he was out of this fight.

I turned to the remaining three... just as the two crossbowmen fired at me.

I tried to move, to spin or drop, but was too slow. I only got out of the way of one. The other hit the outside of my left shoulder and tore a hideous chunk out of my arm.

I screamed, a wild and desperate cry, as I collapsed.

Years of battle training took over. I needed to get up, needed to keep fighting. If I stayed down, stayed still, I was dead.

I gritted my teeth and struggled to rise, managing to get to one knee. But by then, the one man not holding a crossbow had reached me. Behind him, the two crossbowmen had reloaded, fingers on triggers, in case I tried anything.

The man standing over me was the sergeant who'd reminded the others of their orders: kill everyone. His eyes held no mercy as he raised his sword dispassionately.

GLOSSARY

CURRENCY

- ¼ bronze piece – "A Quarter"
- ½ bronze piece – "A Cut Piece"
- bronze coin – "A Sail"
- small silver bar – "A Slip" (=10 sails)
- large silver bar – "A Strip" (=10 slips)
- gold coin – "A Royal" (=50 strips)
- gold bar – "A Bar" (=50 royals)

PLACES OF NOTE

Aestria

Eastern Continent

(Ancient Aestria / Aestrian Empire)

A massive empire over the entire continent. Over

the last thousand years the empire has been in decline – devouring natural resources – many regions starving while the larger cities and the capital grew more opulent. There were many revolts and uprisings. About two hundred years ago, a merchant ship, blown off course in a storm, found its way to Valterra. This began a mass exodus of ships and settlers which sought to leave the empire and settle new kingdoms. Aestria sent merchants and workers to harvest the natural resources of Valterra to return to Aestria, but most of them simply stayed and few resources returned to the empire. Over the last century and a half, the empire fractured into small city-stakes and king-doms, stuck in the old ways.

The Narrow Sea

Separates Aestria from Valterra

Despite its name it isn't a quick trip across – from the narrowest point it takes about two days to cross, but few take that route as it's far to the north and the strong winds which make the trip quick also make it treacherous. Most sail calmer waters to the south, where it takes anywhere from four to six days to cross in calm weather. Pearlia to Therist (Aestrian city) takes about three to five days depending on winds.

Valterra

Western Continent

Inhabited by Dathi and Usovi peoples in the
south and barbarian tribes, north of the Valterran
Mountains. Roughly two hundred years ago
peoples from Aestria came across the Narrow Sea
to settle here.

Usura / Usurn Wilds / The Wildlands
South of continent – a desert and badlands,
farther south is a dense jungle. Home of Usovi
People. Some remain nomadic, others settled
areas of rich resources.

Dathi Lands
The lush mid-region of Valterra, now mostly
settled by Aestrians. Dathi were a nomadic
people, most of whom were friendly and many
settled among the Aestrian cities. A few, purists,
stuck to the old ways. The Purists began a war of
genocide to eradicate all "impure" mixed-blood
Dathi, but the mixed-blood were aided by the
aestrian cities and quickly overwhelmed the
Purists.

Pearlia
Oldest of the Aestrian settled kingdoms in
Valterra, sitting along the Pearline River on the
Narrow Sea. The river had been known as the
Hanoea River by the Dathi previously. Possesses a

deep protected harbor, abundant with oysters and pearls (hence the name)

Three Rings:

The Inner Ring / Old City – where the first settlers landed and built original city.

The Second Ring – originally the park-like estates of noblemen outside of the city. A second wall was built to protect these lands.

Third Ring – the peasant community outside the wall, taller buildings over narrow alleys with few wide roads. A third wall was erected to protect this area, completed roughly twenty years ago

Outside the city slums nestle close to the wall and farther out a caravansary and market of trade goods has sprung up, since many foreign merchants cannot gain access to the city. New Nobles estates have been built outside the walls along the river

Eromore

On the Erovan River, in the North of Valterra, where lands are not as fertile as Pearlia. Have spent generations building their armies to protect from invading barbarians in the north. Recent turned their attentions south to Pearlia.

Vestrea – a southern province of Eromore – war between Eromore and Pearlia divided it up – the bulk staying in Eromore, with the capital and some surrounding southern lands going to Pearlia.

Ossara

Further up the Pearline River on Lake Ostri (Originally named Aester Lake by the new residents, but the Dathi called it Oenin. The names combined over time). Proud peoples – the lake is large, but they are landlocked and cannot get to sea without going through Pearlia – have always had a decent relationship with Pearlia.

Rolvan

South of Pearlia on the edge of the dessert and wilds. Rolvan is a trade city, where Dathi and Usovi come from the west and south to exchange wares. Aestrian, Dathi, and Usovi alike often venture into the dessert and wilds to find ancient (sometimes mystical) artifacts of a lost civilization.

Myrna

Farthest west kingdom, at the edge of settled lands in Valterra, a small kingdom, growing slowly. Trade with still nomadic Dathi who move through the western woods

PEARLIAN ROYAL FAMILY

King Edward Pearlece
Died 7 years ago

Queen Helena Pearlece
Ruling

Prince Victor Pearlece
    Heir apparent
    Married to Princess Kira of Ossara
    Daughter Princess Anastasia (14)
    Daughter Princess Helena (11)
    Son Prince Wilhelm (8)

Princess Beatrice / Queen Beatrice
    Married to King Tharin of Rolvan
    Son Prince Fredrin (16)
    Son Prince Edric (14)
    Son Prince Nikalas (11)

Princess Alice Pearlece
    Never married

Prince Henry Pearlece
    Married to Lady Miraline Highwald
    Son Prince Alfran (8)
    Daughter Princess Gwendolyn (4)

Prince Leonin Pearlece
    Married to Lady Theodora of Vestrea who died 4
years ago
    No children

GODS AND RELIGIONS

Aestrian Deities

Aestric

> Father Deity – Ruler of the Heavens
> God of Rulership, Law, Justice

Assa

> Mother Deity – Queen of the Heavens
> Goddess of Creation, Rebirth, Mercy

Brovos

> God of War and Victory

Halea

> Goddess of Love, Sensuality, Fertility

Wisteri

> Goddess of Knowledge and Learning

Olerin

> God of Cultivation, Agriculture, Husbandry

Lenara

> Goddess of Nature, Wild Animals, Freedom

Dathi & Usovi Deities

Moena

> The Creator
> Neither / Both Genders
> Took a part of themselves to create the world

The Children of Moena

The Dathi and Usovi believe all the peoples of the world are the children of Moena. Moena also created Great Spirits (demi-gods) to help rule over specific domains:

Suoma – The Land
"God" of Protection, Strength

Evos – The Great Waters (seas/lakes)
"Goddess" of Love, Fertility

Kuso – The Lesser Waters (rivers and streams)
Son of Suoma and Evos
"God" of Travel, Journeys, Trade

Ohan – Forests and Jungles
Son of Suoma and Evos
"God" of Wildlife

Apa – The Sun
"God" of Knowledge

Kihuana – The Sky (sometimes light, sometimes dark & stary)
"Goddess" of Secrets

Tawandi – The Wind & Storm
Daughter of Apa and Kihuana
"Goddess" of Fate, Change

Nalo – Fire

Son of Ohan and Tawandi (lightning striking trees)
"God" of Chance, Desire

Datha – The Great Wolf
Dathi peoples are named after him

Uso – The Great Bear
Usovi peoples are named after her

Don't miss the next book in the series!

Sword Skirt
Lady Blade: Book 2

**A man I once hated, a nobleman, and a dear friend all
want to be with me, as if one man wasn't enough!**

My life has been turned upside down. Kelric, my old
flame turned most hated rival is now back in my life and
we have so much lost time to make up for. Yet I've also
gotten quite serious with Leo, the nobleman I'm training
in combat. It can't last between us with him being a
noble, but I intend to make the most of the time we have.

Leo also found me more students and I now have a

cohort of young women who want to learn to protect themselves. I love working with the Sword Skirts (their name not mine) and I'll never be able to thank Leo enough for bringing them into my life.

Oh, and Dazar, who I've known almost my entire life, has confessed his love for me. I'm still getting used to that idea, but when he sweeps me up in his magical aura and touches me like no other man can it's hard to say no.

And with attacks on the prince and his mistress thrown into the mix, I'm all turned around. I don't know what to do, but for the moment I have three men who love me and I'll take that for as long as I can. Who knows, maybe I won't have to choose between them?

OTHER BOOKS BY CLARA WILS

Fantasy Reverse Harem

THE MISTS OF ELISTA TRILOGY

Bonds and Blood, book 1

Shape and Shadows, book 2

Form and Fury, book 3

THE SISTER SPIRITS SERIES

Double Discover, book 1

Double Danger, book 2

Double Disaster, book 3

Double Doom, book 4

Double Destiny, book 5

Portal Fantasy Reverse Harem

THE GRECIAN GODDESS TRILOGY

co-written with Tessa Cole

Kiss of the Goddess, book 1

Power of the Goddess, book 2

Bonds of the Goddess, book 3

Paranormal Reverse Harem

THE SECRETS GODS KEEP TRILOGY

co-written with Tessa Cole

Craving Demons, book 1

Chaos Demons, book 2

Claiming Demons, book 3

HER BAD BOY WOLVE TRILOGY

co-written with Tessa Cole

Pack To The Wall, book 1

Want You Pack, book 2

Pack In Business, book 3